23.95

S0-AGT-707

THE SWAMPS OF BAYOU TECHE

A Tony Boudreaux Mystery

THE SWAMPS OF
BAYOU TECHE

•

Kent Conwell

AVALON BOOKS
NEW YORK

MYS

Published by Thomas Bouregy & Co., Inc.
160 Madison Avenue, New York, NY 10016

Library of Congress Cataloging-in-Publication Data

Conwell, Kent.
    The Swamps of Bayou Teche / Kent Conwell.
        p. cm.
    ISBN 978-0-8034-9858-7 (acid-free paper) 1. Swamps—
Fiction. 2. Murder—Investigation—Fiction. 3. Louisiana—
Fiction. I. Title.

    PS3553.O547S93 2007
    813'.54—dc22

                                            2007016635

PRINTED IN THE UNITED STATES OF AMERICA
ON ACID-FREE PAPER
BY HADDON CRAFTSMEN, BLOOMSBURG, PENNSYLVANIA

To Amy, who always fusses she never gets a book dedicated to her without my wife's name in the dedication also. This one is it.
I love you, Amy.
Dad

Chapter One

"*C'est mon cauchemar*! This is my nightmare."

If I heard that old expression once while I was growing up, I heard it a thousand times. An idiom in the oral tradition of Nova Scotia, the exiled Acadians carried it with them throughout the dispersal to Louisiana beginning in the eighteenth century. The word itself, cauchemar, sometimes meant nightmare; sometimes, it meant witches, both evil and good.

Whatever it meant at the moment, the avowal was usually uttered by superstitious old Acadians, blaming the misery of a restless or sleepless night on the curses of evil witches, or cauchemars.

Folklore had it that the cauchemars made Cajun women spin and knit and weave all night long. The myths also warned that cauchemars turned men into horses and rode them through the bottoms, through bogs and swamps. And in the morning when the Cajun awakened feeling all worn out and "hag-ridden," he would exclaim, *"C'est mon cauchemar!* I had a nightmare."

Naturally, I didn't believe in curses or the old stories, nor the eerie ones about the Jack-O-Lanterns that led the unsuspecting victim deep into the unfathomable swamps along the Bayou Teche, nor the whispers of the devilish *coquin l'eau* or the *feu follet,* nor the hushed stories of the innocent men turned into *loup garous,* unfortunate beings that take the shapes of various animals and roam the swamps during the dark of the moon.

Still, it's unsettling how so unexpectedly the phobias, the fears, the fright of youth can come back to haunt a person—just like last spring when my boss, Marty Blevins, called me into his office and announced that I was heading back to Louisiana on a missing-person caper.

The hair on the back of my neck bristled, not from fear, but from anger.

Missing persons was the bailiwick of neophyte P.I.'s, and I was years beyond that. At the time I was egotistical enough to figure such an assignment was like hitching a thoroughbred to a breaking plow. "Find someone else, Marty. What about your cousin over in Baton Rouge? He's always after you for a gig. I'm tied up with the insurance scam at National Life and Guaranty."

He shrugged. "Untie yourself then. This old lady is paying more than enough to cover your salary for the next three months. Besides, that cousin of mine is a lying jerk."

I rolled my eyes. I had just lost my argument. Money drove Marty, and I knew I had no chance in winning a dispute with him when he was holding a poker hand worth three months of my salary. I responded with a pointed quip, "That's means I get a raise, huh?"

"Besides," he added, ignoring my witty repartee, "you're from the swamps over in Louisiana. You know those people. You'll feel right at home with the gumbo mud squeezing up between your toes." His chair protested with squeaks and groans when he leaned back and gave me a smug grin at what I suppose he considered a humorous retort to my question.

I stared at him, not laughing. He wouldn't know gumbo mud from concrete. The phone rang before I could respond. Marty grabbed at the receiver, jammed it in his ear, and mumbled unintelligibly. Finally, he nodded. "Certainly, Mrs. Hardy. Come right on up." He cut his eyes up to me. "We'll be waiting in my private office." He replaced the receiver and gestured to a chair. "Sit. That was our Louisiana client. She's coming right up." He struggled to button the collar around his fleshy neck, but quickly gave up and tightened his tie.

Frowning, I sat. I wasn't crazy about driving back

to Louisiana. I'd been there a couple months earlier to visit family, so I hadn't planned on a return trip until late summer. "What are we doing with a Louisiana client? I might be mistaken," I replied, sarcasm coating my words thicker than cane syrup from St. Landry Parish. "Last I heard, they do have private security agencies in Louisiana."

Marty grunted. "She's an old lady. She lives here in Austin. She says her boy's missing. She wants us to find him. And she's loaded. I checked," he added smugly, with a gleam in his eye.

That still didn't answer my question, but before I could reply, an elderly woman wearing bright pink sweats and carrying a lime green purse bounded through the front door, paused, looked around, and when she spotted us through the office door, waved and strode across the room.

Her white hair was neatly coiffed, and from what I could tell, not a strand was out of place. She appeared frail enough to be ninety, but she moved with the ease of a forty-year old.

I opened the door to Marty's office as she drew near.

She beamed up at me. "Thank you, young man," she said in a soft, cultured voice. "That's very sweet of you. It is gratifying to see that there are still some gentlemen left," she added, cutting her blue eyes sharply toward Marty, who remained slouched in his chair.

By the time he recognized the implication in her remark and struggled to lift his bulk to his feet, the tiny lady had seated herself primly in one of the chairs in front of his desk. Red-faced, he cleared his throat. "Mrs. Hardy?"

She nodded sharply. "Mrs. Josepphine Hardy, with two p's, Mr. Blevins." Then in short, terse words that rat-tat-tatted like a machine gun, which told me she was used to having her way, she proceeded to tell us that her son had not returned to work at his bank in Bagotville on Bayou Teche, south of Lafayette. With a sniff, she added, "Of course you might not know, but Bagotville was named after my ancestor, Lucien Bagot, who settled the area along the Teche in the early nineteenth century, 1821 to be exact. My husband and I left Bagotville forty years ago. We were thrilled when Johnny wanted to go back."

Marty and I glanced at each other. I arched an eyebrow. He frowned at me.

She continued. "My boy had been turkey hunting down by Morgan City, Mr. Blevins," she explained. "He was due back at his bank last Monday, but he didn't return."

Turkey hunting? Morgan City? I'd never heard about turkeys around Morgan City, but then I'd been away from Louisiana for years except for occasional visits. I glanced at Marty skeptically, then cleared my throat. "How old is your son, Mrs. Hardy?"

Without hesitation, she replied, "Fifty-seven."

Fifty-seven! I arched an eyebrow at Marty and made an half-hearted effort to allay her concerns. "He probably decided to stay over, Mrs. Hardy." I really wanted to say "hey, the guy's almost sixty-years old. He can take care of himself," but I didn't. Her distress was obvious.

"Did he notify anyone he would be staying over? Perhaps his wife."

She sniffed and drew herself erect. "Johnny isn't married. He could never find the right woman. He did call his secretary, but I don't believe her," she snapped.

Now she had me confused. Her son told his secretary he would not return as planned, and yet his mother still believed something was wrong. "What did he say to her? His secretary, I mean."

She fixed her cold blue eyes on me. "That he was going to the Bahamas."

I pursed my lips. "Then that must be where he is. Don't you think so? Or do you think his secretary lied about his whereabouts."

Her eyes narrowed. "No, Mr.—" She frowned. "What is your name, young man?" She cut her eyes accusingly at Marty. "We haven't been properly introduced."

Marty's cheeks turned red, and my ears burned as I replied, "Boudreaux, Mrs. Hardy. Tony Boudreaux."

She nodded in satisfaction. "No, Mr. Boudreaux. I do not believe he went to the Bahamas," she replied, emphasizing "do not." "In fact, I am positive he did not, but in all fairness to Ms. Palmo—that's his secretary—I do not believe she lied."

Marty cleared his throat. "I don't—I mean, we

don't understand, Mrs. Hardy. If you don't think she lied, then why don't you believe your son went to the Bahamas?"

With a touch of exasperation, she explained, "Because Johnny always tells me where he is going. He knows how I worry about him, so even though he lives over four hundred miles away, he e-mails or calls when he is away from Bagotville." Her eyes flickered with impatience when she saw the amusement in my own eyes. "For your information, I have a heart condition, Mr. Boudreaux. Johnny knows that a sudden shock could cause me problems. That's why he keeps me informed."

Her explanation embarrassed me. I nodded. "I apologize, Mrs. Hardy." I paused. "We can look into it for you, ma'am, but, why us? It would cost you considerably less if you retained a local agency near Morgan City."

"Because, Mr. Boudreaux," she replied, her icy blue eyes fixed on mine, "I don't trust anyone I can't confront to face to face. I don't mind driving about Austin, but I'm too old to drive to Louisiana." Studying me a moment, she shifted her piercing gaze on Marty. "I'm a pragmatist, Mr. Blevins. My son is missing. I want him found, one way or another."

The tone in her voice when she said "one way or another" piqued my curiosity. Before I could respond, she continued, her eyes defiant. "Johnny has made enemies in his business. Banking, gentlemen, is not a gentleman's business. Hard, impersonal decisions must be made, and consequently, over the years, some tragedies do occur. My own husband, Johnny's father, was a banker. An irate investor shot and killed him."

Marty frowned at me, clearly confused. I wasn't much better off, but at least I managed to stammer out a question. "What are you trying to say?"

"Just this. My son is missing. I want him found. If he has been hurt or . . ." She paused, tears glittering in the corner of her cold blue eyes. She cleared her throat. "Or worse, then I will triple your fee to find those responsible."

Before I could respond, she opened that lime green purse and extracted a matching lime green checkbook. She cut her eyes to Marty, and in a cool, businesslike voice, stated, "Will ten thousand be enough of a retainer, Mr. Blevins?"

Without giving him a chance to respond, she briskly wrote out the check, fished a small cassette and a snapshot from her purse, and handed them to Marty. "I know you people always want background about your subjects. At least, that's what I see on television. I have all the pertinent information you need about Johnny to start your investigation."

"Just a moment, Mrs. Hardy," I hastily interjected. "If something has happened to your son, that will be a matter for the local law enforcement agencies. We can't simply walk in and investigate any infractions of the law."

Nodding briefly, she replied, "I know, but I also know you people can always find a way around the law." With that, she rose, smiled brightly at each of us, and strode from the office.

When she closed the office door behind her, Marty and I exchanged expressions of weary relief. "I feel like a steamroller just ran over me," I muttered.

"Yeah," he muttered back.

I eyed him threateningly. "I hope you don't plan on me doing more than a missing persons on this case. I don't want to get crossways with the Louisiana law."

He shrugged. "Stay legal." He waved the check. "Play it by ear. You can't tell what will happen."

"As long as you understand," I replied, stepping to the window and peering down into the parking lot.

Marty didn't answer. In the reflection from the window, I saw him staring greedily at the ten-thousand-dollar check in his hand. I could almost see the drool running down the side of his lips.

"Would you look at that," I mumbled, taken aback when Mrs. Josepphine "with two p's" Hardy climbed into a cherry red Jaguar XK Roadster.

By the time Marty reached my side, the spry little lady had pulled onto Lamar and was racing north.

We watched silently as she wove through the traffic skillfully. With his eyes still fixed on the Jag, Marty handed me the cassette and snapshot. "When do you plan on leaving?"

Without taking my eyes off the red bullet speeding down the crowded thoroughfare, I replied, "Soon as I can. Maybe I can beat the afternoon traffic jams."

He grunted. "Six one way, half-dozen the other. Miss the Austin jams, you catch the Houston jams."

I couldn't argue with that nugget of wisdom anymore than he could argue with ten thousand dollars.

After the little sports car disappeared, I turned to Marty, and tapped the corner of the card-sized cassette against the palm of my hand. "I have a funny feeling about this case, Marty."

He shrugged and folded the check into his shirt pocket. "Probably those Tex-Mex burritos you had for breakfast. Now, get home and pack. The sooner you get over there, the sooner you'll get back."

I stared at him, and for some inexplicable, but foreboding reason, the words "c'est mon cauchemar" flashed through my mind.

On the way to my place on Peyton Gin Road, I listened to a portion of the tape, ejecting it when I reached the apartment and playing the remainder of it while I packed a sports bag and gathered the rest of my gear.

I still couldn't get over the feeling that something wasn't quite right. And it wasn't the Tex-Mex burritos.

Chapter Two

J ust as I dumped ice around the Old Milwaukee beer in my small cooler, the doorbell chimed. I opened it to the grinning face of my one-time teaching pal, Jack Edney, burr haircut and all—a nouveau millionaire who had just lost his campaign for city council, a campaign, which I am ashamed to admit, I had managed for him. (I still think if he'd taken my advice and let his hair grow, he would have won the election. For some reason, bald-headed fat men turn off voters. Probably because they look like bankers.)

He barged inside. "Hey, Tony. What's up?" He spotted my sports bag and the open cooler on the couch. "Going somewhere?"

I snapped the cooler lid in place. "Louisiana. Got a

client over there, and I was just leaving," I added, hoping he would take the hint.

He did, but not the way I expected. "Louisiana? Great! How about company? Or is Janice going?"

Janice Coffman-Morrison was my on-again, off-again significant other. What prompted his question is that Janice had once decided she wanted to partner with me in the P.I. business. One case, and she backed out. Probably because three triad goons came within ten seconds of burying us in another guy's grave.

Before I could reply, he prodded me. "Huh? Is she?"

That's when I made my first mistake. I replied before I thought. "No. She decided she wasn't cut out for the private eye business."

Jack grinned. "Fantastic. So then what about me, Tony? I could use a break after the campaign. You need the company."

I hesitated, which was my second mistake.

He begged, "Come on, Tony. Please. I need to get away for a while. Diane is driving me nuts."

Diane was my ex-wife who had shown up in Austin the year before and hooked up with Jack. She worked for the National Park Service at L.B.J.'s boyhood home over in Johnson City, Texas, and rented one of the apartments in Jack's complex on Austin's west side.

I looked around at him, surprised.

He nodded emphatically. "I've never seen a woman spend money like she does, and if I don't buy her every little thing she wants, she pouts." He shook his head wearily. "And believe me, she has pouting down to a science. Honest to Pete, Tony. I need a break, big time."

Pausing to collect my thoughts, I nodded to his burgeoning belly beneath his garish Hawaiian shirt. "You're putting on weight."

A rueful grin played over his fleshy cheeks. "Diane. The woman thrives on steak and wine, pasta and wine, anything and wine. She doesn't gain an ounce, but I've put on thirty pounds this past year." He shook his head. "I'm up to a forty-six in my slacks, and I don't even wear Levis anymore," he said, gesturing to the washed-out Levis I wore. "You ever see a fat man in Levis? It's obscene. If this keeps up, I'll be forced to start wearing muumuu Levis."

I arched an eyebrow, trying to imagine muumuu Levis. I shook my head and with a grin, replied, "Just don't get a red one. Red isn't your color."

He muttered a derogatory epithet. "Well, can I?"

For a moment, I studied the plaintive expression on his face. It reminded me of my grandfather's Bluetick hound. With a sigh of resignation, I shook my head. "How soon can you get packed?"

A grin wider than the Mississippi River split his face. "I'm ready now. I'll call my apartment manager and tell him. I can pick up what I need along the way. And, hey," he added, "let's go in my Cadillac. I just bought a new convertible."

"A new one? You bought one only six months ago."

"Yeah, but Diane didn't like the color."

All I could do was roll my eyes. Better him than me. "Grab the ice chest then."

He hesitated, eyeing the ice chest skeptically. "Beer?"

I looked around. "Yeah. Why?"

"I thought you were on the wagon. You know, A.A."

"I am on the wagon. An occasional beer won't hurt."

He hesitated, frowning. "Hey, I don't know about the beer, Tony. If you're on the wagon, then—"

"Look, Jack," I snapped. "There's wagons and then there's wagons. This is my little red wagon. Now, are you going with me or not?"

With a gleeful chuckle, he grabbed the ice chest and scooted out the door. I paused in the doorway, looking over my apartment. For the first time in years, I didn't have to worry about pets.

Oscar, my Albino Barb exotic fish, had died a few months before, and Cat, the kitten that had taken his place for a few days had vanished as mysteriously as he had appeared. I was pet-free and intended to remain that way.

"Climb in," he said, nodding to the Cadillac. "Just throw the junk on the seat in back."

In addition to a couple changes of clothes, my junk included a laptop, a portable printer, and a small bag of tools, tools I would have a hard time explaining to any law officer if he found them in my possession. The fact I was a private investigator was no excuse for possession of burglary paraphernalia.

While I preferred driving pickups, the luxury of Jack's Cadillac XLR with the 4.6L V8 engine and five-speed automatic could spoil a person in a big hurry. So luxurious was the vehicle that even the clutter of wadded Kleenexes, gum wrappers, and crushed beer cans on the floor didn't faze me.

Before we pulled away from the curb in front of my apartment, he lowered the top and grinned at me. "Might as well enjoy the sun."

I grinned back at him, and in Clint Eastwood's inimitable manner, I pointed my finger east and muttered, "Forward!"

As we sped along Highway 290 from Austin to Houston, I briefly told Jack about the case, and then for the next few hundred miles, listened to the cassette.

To my surprise, I learned that John Hardy, Johnny as his mother called him, didn't simply work at the bank in Bagotville. He owned it with a partner, Marvin Gates. Although Hardy and Gates were not personal friends, as partners the two were ideal counterpoints for each other. And, if the cassette were to be believed, Hardy was Mr. Bagotville—but then, mothers generally have a tendency to view their offspring through the proverbial rose-colored glasses.

By the time I listened to the tape the third time, I knew the missing man was a major player in the community as well as an entrepreneurial businessman who refused to permit past failures to slow him down.

In other words, John Hardy never allowed anyone or any problem stand in his way. Of course, I reminded myself this was only his mother's perspective, and mothers do have a tendency to gloss over their offspring's bad habits.

That night Jack and I took separate rooms at the Live Oaks Motel in Lafayette, Louisiana. Now, I'm not a particularly fastidious or picky person, but Jack is the consummate slob.

So later that evening, while I sat in my quiet room working on an itinerary for the coming day, I could hear the TV blasting from his room next door. And I knew if I popped over there, I would find him sprawled in bed scarfing down multi-topping pizza, gulping beer, and watching X-rated movies on pay TV.

In developing my itinerary, the last thing on my mind was that John Hardy might be dead.

Chapter Three

When I reached Bagotville next morning, the first person I planned to see was John Hardy's girl Friday, his secretary. I glanced at my notes taken from the cassette Mrs. Hardy had provided. Laura Palmo was the secretary's name.

Bagotville was some fifty miles south of Lafayette between Centerville and Calumet, a picture postcard town of neat brick homes, moss-draped trees, and a well-manicured park on the banks of the lazy Bayou Teche.

"Pretty little town," Jack observed as we drove past the city limit sign shaded by an ancient live oak with branches over fifty feet long and Spanish moss dangling almost to the ground.

"Yep." I pointed to a Texaco service station. "Pull in over there. Let's fill up."

"I just filled up back in Lafayette."

"I want to find out where the bank is."

Jack topped off the tank while I went inside. The smell of fish smacked me in the face. A tiny woman with sun-weathered wrinkles, twinkling brown eyes, and a friendly smile appeared in an open door behind the counter. "Morning," she said, coming into the room while drying her hands on a soiled orange towel. "Don't be minding the smell. Me, I be bagging craw-fish my old man, Tiburse, he bring in." She shook her head, her short brown hair bobbing behind. "We be busy this time of year."

"Good morning," I replied, smiling at the unmistak-able Cajun lilt in her voice. "My friend's filling up. We're looking for the local bank."

She arched an eyebrow and her infectious smile grew wider. "Which one? We have two."

"The one John Hardy owns."

She raised her eyebrows. "*Bien!* Mr. Hardy, he be fine man. *Gentilhomme,* you know what I mean?"

My French wasn't so rusty that I couldn't under-stand her. I nodded. "A gentleman."

"*Oui! Ma foi,* a fine man." She pointed out the win-dow. "East side of town square. It be Bagotville Na-tional Bank." She jabbed her middle finger into her chest. "My old man and me, we be customers of Mr. Hardy. He treat us, all of us like we be his own children," she said, making a sweeping gesture with her arm that encompassed the entire village.

Jack came in at that moment. "Didn't take much, only six gallons."

He reached for his wallet, but I stopped him. "I'll get it. I'm on expenses, remember."

Jack flipped open his wallet. "Yeah, but I'm a multi-millionaire, remember? You helped make me one." He pulled out a hundred-dollar bill and offered it to the little Cajun lady. "And keep the change," he added, winking at her.

She stared at the bald pate of Ben Franklin on the bill in disbelief, but only for a brief second before quickly jamming it elbow-deep into her bra before Jack could change his mind. With a crooked grin, she eyed Jack's expansive belly. "You must like the crawfish, hey? You wait. I give you some."

We declined the crawfish, and five minutes later pulled up in front of the Bagotville National Bank. Jack grunted and glanced around the small town. "Right out of 'Gone With the Wind,' " he observed.

I couldn't argue with him there. The red brick and white mortar, as well as the stately columns with intricate Ionic capitals, gave the Bagotville National Bank the look of Tara. Giant live oaks spread throughout the town. Spanish moss swayed from great branches, brushed gently by the warm breezes that carried the sleepy aroma of honeysuckle and jasmine.

I climbed out of the Cadillac. "You coming in?"

"Naw. You go." He gestured to the city square. "Think I'll look around."

"Don't get lost. Depending on what I find out in here, we could be turning around and heading right back home."

Laura Palmo was one of those petite ladies who must have discovered the Fountain of Youth—one of those intriguing women almost impossible to pin an age on. Her raven-black hair fell about her shoulders, combed so the shiny locks draped over her left cheek, giving her the mysterious look of the old B-movie femme fatale. She had the natural slenderness of an eighteen-year-old high school senior, and her complexion, though flawless, was dark, which, complemented by her black eyes, proved striking.

I guessed her dress size was about a four and her age around thirty-five or -six.

She smiled brightly up at me when I stopped in front of her desk. "May I help you?"

I expected more of a Cajun inflection in her voice, the lack of which told me that she, unlike my little friend with the crawfish, had not spent her life in Bagotville. I introduced myself, explaining I was trying to locate John Hardy.

When I mentioned Josepphine Hardy, a weary frown flickered over her face. She closed her eyes and shook her head wearily. A weak smile played over her lips. "I apologize for your trip over, Mr. Boudreaux. I told Mrs. Hardy that John had called from the hunting camp on the twenty-fifth. He and a client decided to take a short jaunt to the Bahamas. He called back two days later from the Bahamas and left a number where he could be reached. He told me to call his mother and inform her, which I did." She sighed. "But since you are here, then obviously Jos—I mean Mrs. Hardy— must not have believed me."

I arched an eyebrow. That was a little tidbit of information Mrs. Hardy had failed to mention. "When does he plan on returning?"

She grimaced. "He didn't say." She paused, and when she spoke, she had slipped into the mantle of secretarial privilege regarding her boss's behavior. "I'm not sure. Sometimes, John—I mean Mr. Hardy—is gone for a week or two."

"So, he has done this before."

Laura Palmo nodded emphatically. "Oh, yes. And Mrs. Hardy is well aware of that," she added, her tone edged with catty impatience.

"Out of curiosity, Ms. Palmo. Did Mr. Hardy have any enemies?"

"Enemies?" A frown wrinkled her forehead. "Why are you asking that? Do you think something's happened to him?"

"Mrs. Hardy suggested the possibility. Me, I don't know. I'm just trying to find him." I gave her a smile that was intended to be disarming. "So, can you think of someone who might have had a grudge against him for whatever reason—being refused a loan, foreclosure—that sort of thing."

She arched an eyebrow and smiled. "People always curse bankers, Mr. Boudreaux. They'll curse them, but usually that's as far as it goes. I've known Josepphine for several years. She's always afraid something will happen to her son." She hesitated, then added, "Probably because of what happened to her husband."

I nodded, understanding her implication. "So he didn't have any enemies that you know of?"

"Not of the sort you mean."

"I see. Now you say he took a client to the Bahamas. Can you tell me who this client is?"

She smiled up at me with pained tolerance. "I can't do that, Mr. Boudreaux. Mr. Hardy would not approve."

I grinned. "It was a shot. How about the phone number in the Bahamas? Can you give me that?"

"Why certainly," she replied briskly, reaching for her address book. She inadvertently knocked over a stack of mail, spilling it on the floor.

"Let me," I said, kneeling to gather the half dozen or so envelopes. Scooping them up, I handed them to her. I noticed the return address on the top envelope was from Antigua. "Here you are."

She smiled shyly, a blush on her cheeks. "Thank you. Now, let me get that number. Like I said, he called from the Bahamas with this number where I could reach him." She jotted it down and handed it to me.

"That was after the hunting trip."

"Yes. It was a spring turkey hunt. A special hunt, John said." She smiled warmly.

"I should have come a little earlier," I replied, with a smile of my own. "I do a little hunting myself."

She arched an eyebrow.

I continued, "I'm not much of a hunter, probably not as good a one as your boss. But I enjoy being outdoors."

Laura Palmo laughed softly. "To be honest, neither is Mr. Hardy. It had been so long since he'd been hunting, he had to go out and buy new clothes, waterproof boots and all."

"Thanks for making me feel better," I replied. "Now, can you tell me the name of the hunting camp near Morgan City? I'll drive down and see what I come up with. Maybe I can get enough to satisfy his mother."

"I hope so," she replied. "It's Benoit's Hunting Lodge down in Terrechoisie Parish. Can't miss it. A big sign this side of Morgan City shows the way." She smiled sadly. "But I hate to see you make the trip for nothing. That's all it will be, a waste of time."

"Have you talked to him since he called?"

She smiled warmly. "No. He instructed me to call only in an emergency."

I believed her. From what I had learned from Laura Palmo, I could see no reason for Mrs. Hardy to worry.

She continued, "But I can understand Josepphine did retain the services of your company and you must fulfill the contract for payment. Money, she make the world go around," she added with an affected Cajun lilt and a charming smile.

I grinned at her sheepishly. "Sounds kind of cold when you put it like that. The money, I mean."

She laughed, a warm, throaty chuckle.

I nodded. "Thanks for the information." I hesitated. "By the way. How long have you worked here for John Hardy?"

Her eyes opened wide in mock surprise. She pressed one hand to the base of her throat, and a wildly exaggerated Southern-belle drawl, said, "Why, is little old me under suspicion, Mr. Boudreaux?"

"Of course not." I laughed. "And call me Tony."

"All right, Tony. I'm Laura. I've been here nine years. Mr. Hardy hired me in '96 into the secretarial pool. Then four years ago, I became Mr. Hardy's and Mr. Gate's personal secretary."

"You're not from around here though."

She hesitated for only a fleeting moment, just as fleeting as the tiny frown that knit an eyebrow.

I continued, "You don't have the accent of the natives."

Laughing, she nodded. "You're right. From up north. Minneapolis. Grew tired of the cold and ended up here. And I don't plan on ever going back, despite the hurricanes that come through every once in a while," she added.

I glanced around, then lowered my voice, "You've known Mrs. Hardy for four years, you say?" She nodded, and I continued, "Well, something's been puzzling me about her."

Laura, with an arch of an eyebrow, replied wryly, "Josepphine puzzles a lot of people." She slapped her fingers to her lips. "I didn't say that," she whispered, her eyes laughing.

"And I didn't hear it."

"So, what about her?"

I blurted out, "Why are there two p's in her name?"

She studied me a moment, then rolled her eyes. "That's just her. You know this town is named after one of their ancestors." I nodded, and she continued, "From what I heard, over forty years ago, she decided that since she was not a common person, her name should not be spelled as such. So—" She arched her eyebrows as if to say, "that's why."

"And that's it, huh?"

"That's it. At least, that's what Mr. Hardy told me. Just an affectation, nothing more." She paused a moment, a quizzical arch to her eyebrows and a crooked smile on her lips, "Satisfied?"

I shrugged. "I suppose." I studied her a moment, and with a wry grin, replied, "Makes you wonder why someone would do something like that."

She gave me a look that screamed you've-got-to-be-kidding. "You've met her. Why do you think? By the way, is she still driving her white Mercedes convertible?"

"Mercedes?" I shook my head, then chuckled as I

understood just what Laura Palmo was implying. "She was tooling through Austin traffic in a cherry red Jag Roadster last time I saw her."

Laura held her hands out to her sides. "I rest my case. She really is a sweet old lady, but she likes to be noticed and wants to keep her son tied to her apron strings. That's the real reason she hired you."

I glanced at the notes in my hand. "Like you said, the trip on down to Morgan City is probably a waste of time."

By the time I reached the glass doors at the front of the bank, I had made up my mind to head back to Austin. There was nothing here except a worried mother. I glanced back across the lobby at Laura Palmo behind the railing separating her desk from the lobby. She smiled and waved. I waved back, and as I left the bank, I glanced at the telephone number she had given me. The Dolphin Bay Country Club at Freeport on Grand Bahama. Telephone 1-800-739-xxxx, room 417.

I would call John Hardy and insist he contact his mother. And then my job was done.

Folding the sheet of paper into my shirt pocket, I started down the sidewalk to the Cadillac.

Then I froze.

Hastily, I fumbled in my pocket for the paper with Hardy's telephone number. I reread it, then stared off into space, mixed thoughts tumbling through my head.

But foremost was the idea that perhaps the trip to Morgan City might not be a waste of time after all— that perhaps there was more to this case than simply a doddering old woman wanting to keep her son tied to her apron strings.

I pulled out my cell phone and punched in the telephone number Laura had given me. I listened carefully as the operator at the Dolphin Bay Country Club in the Bahamas answered. After a moment, I said, "I beg your pardon. I have the wrong number."

For several seconds, I stared at the small silver phone. Now I knew something was wrong.

To confirm the gut feeling nagging at me, I called information, then once again Dolphin Bay Country Club. I asked for room 417. Moments later, I hung up, my gut feeling verified.

First stop—Benoit's Hunting Lodge, Morgan City, Louisiana.

Chapter Four

Jack started the engine as I slammed the door. "Where now? Back home?" He grunted.

I hooked my thumb south. "Morgan City."

A sly grin slid over his rotund face as he backed out of the parking slot. "Found something, huh?"

"I'm not sure," I replied with a shrug. "But maybe down there, I can make two plus two add up to four."

He just nodded and gunned the engine. The powerful car leaped forward, heading for Morgan City on Highway 87, the scenic route, tagged by the state as the Bayou Teche Scenic Byway.

Not only could Jack live with absolute nonchalance in the squalor of empty beer cans and greasy boxes filled with pizza crumbs, he also was blessed with an intellectual curiosity equaled only by a toad frog. So the fact he didn't ask me to explain what I had discovered to send us on down to Morgan City gave me time to sort my thoughts while we sped down the quaint road, lined with mossy trees and dark, deep swamps.

I didn't have much information, but what little I had only took a few minutes to organize. First, Hardy had not returned on schedule. Second, the last verifiable time he had been seen was at Benoit's Hunting Lodge. And third, he was not at Dolphin Bay.

The wind was blowing my hair, and the warm sun chased off the last of the night chill of the swamps. I scooted around in the seat. "Are you wondering why we're going on down to Morgan City?"

Jack shrugged. "Not particularly."

I couldn't help grinning, imagining just what shape our world would be in if everyone possessed Jack's unquenchable thirst for knowledge. "You know, I told you this guy was supposed to be in the Bahamas."

"Yeah, but his old lady doesn't think he is." He looked around at me.

I nodded. "Well, she was right. He isn't. At least, not where he's supposed to be."

"Huh?" He frowned at me. "How did you find that out?"

"Keep your eyes on the road, and I'll tell you. It was simple. I called. John Hardy isn't registered at the hotel where he said he was going to stay. He was supposed to be in room four seventeen, but there isn't a four seventeen."

He glanced at me, a puzzled frown on his face. "Didn't his old lady have the number? Why didn't she call?"

I shrugged. "I long ago gave up trying to figure out the fairer sex."

"So what made you decide to call?"

"The phone number his secretary gave me." I read it off to him. "One, eight hundred, seven-three-nine . . . room four one seven."

He gave me a blank stared and shrugged. "So what's the big deal?"

"So, for hotel chains, eight hundred and eight eighty-eight exchanges are usually informational and reservation numbers. Stop and think. Have you ever called an eight hundred number to reach an individual's room in a hotel?"

Nodding slowly as the explanation sunk in, he said. "So, when you—Hey! Look at that, would you? That city limits sign."

I looked around in the direction he was pointing. A large sign by the side of the macadam road announced the city limits of Maida, Home of the Bayou Teche Loup Garou Festival! At the bottom of the sign was a caricature of a sway-backed horse chewing on a fence.

Jack shook his head. "What are they talking about? What's a loup garou?"

Laughing I explained that it was an old French

myth. "Supposedly it claims that witches can change men into animals."

He rolled his eyes and flexed his fingers about the steering wheel. "Like a werewolf, huh?"

"Not exactly," I replied, remembering stories from the old ones whispered around a fireplace on cold winter nights out on the Louisiana prairies. "Different animals. Not all loup garous were bad. I remember one story about a white eagle loup garou."

"A what?" He responded in disbelief, thinking I was pulling his leg.

"White eagle. The way the story went was this man was gone from his family for a long time. He wanted to see them, so a witch turned him into an eagle so he could fly back and see his wife and children, which he did. Men are turned into horses or cows or just about anything. Whatever the witch decides."

Jack blew out through his lips. "Weird. You know, these people are weird. Nice and friendly, but weird." He paused, then added, "I don't know about you, but I'm hungry."

"Then find us a place to stop," I said, nodding to the little town ahead of us.

Later, a mile beyond the Maida city limits, we passed the Louisianne Casino on Highway 182. A few miles farther, we found the sign marking the turnoff to Benoit's Hunting Lodge, exactly where Laura Palmo had said it would be. I expected a clamshell road, but instead a narrow macadam road twisted back through the cypress and wateroaks of a vast swamp sprawling over several hundred square miles between the Intra-Coastal Canal and Highway 182.

The brown water of the swamp lapped at the edges of the asphalt road. The thick shadows cast by the canopy of leaves overhead held in the heat rising from the earth. The appearance of a swamp is deceiving, not cool as perceived, but instead suffocating, for there is no breeze to stir the air, to dissipate the heat. And the fetid stench of the tepid water clogs the nostrils.

After a few miles, we emerged from the trees into a sea of water cane ten feet tall, lining the road on either side as far ahead as the eye could see. The macadam road made a wide curve to the left and then twisted into several smaller dipsy-doodle curves.

Jack grunted. "Sure hate to have car trouble out here." He paused. "Think there's many alligators around?"

I laughed. "Think dogs got fleas?"

He gulped.

Jack whistled when we pulled up in front of Benoit's Hunting Lodge. I was just as surprised, for instead of a weathered camp with rundown buildings and a battered fleet of aluminum boats, we were staring at a well-maintained two-story lodge constructed of logs perched several feet above the water, on H-bar piers sunk in concrete.

Beneath the lodge gently rocked a fleet of camouflaged boats that appeared to be equipped with the latest in technology.

But what was even more surprising was the obviously affluent clientele. I spotted a Hummer, three extended cab pickups, and a Lexus, all new. In fact, one of the extended cabs still had the dealer's license in the rear window. Parked at the side of the lot were the lodge vehicles, three four-wheel drive GMC extended cab pickups, two Cadillac sedans, and four Jeeps, all painted white with identical logos depicting a hunter pulling down on an incoming brace of ducks.

"Fancy," Jack muttered.

"Yeah," I whispered.

Inside, the accommodations were on the second floor, which was reached by a broad staircase hewn from great logs. If the room appointments were as elaborate as the furniture and decorations on the first floor, then I figured they were way too pricey for a P.I.'s salary.

Charley Benoit and his wife, Marie, were amiable, down-to-earth Cajuns, having worked for twenty years to build the lodge from a single shack to one that catered to a dozen clients daily and was booked up for the next eighteen months.

The permanent grin on Charley's weather-worn face faded when I mentioned John Hardy. "*Mais fois,* do I remember that one." He shook his head and blew through his lips. "He be nothing but trouble."

Clearing his throat, Jack pointed to the bar. "If you don't mind, Tony, while you're busy here, I'll be busy over there."

I waved him in that direction. "Now, how's that, Mr. Benoit? What kind of trouble?"

"That one, he don't come to hunt the turkey. He don't even bring no boots. He gots to buy some from our store. He come to drink and mess with the lady. He don't like to go in the boat to the blinds on the prairie."

"Lady? What lady is that?"

"The one he come with. Cullen be her name. Sue Cullen. She owns some business in Maida." He paused and frowned up at me. "Why you ask all these questions?"

I quickly explained why I was there.

He nodded. "Gone, huh? You think he be dead?"

His question surprised me. "I don't know. Do you?"

"Who can say? He cause fight. Big argument."

"Fight? With who?"

"He fight with just about everyone. This Cullen woman, she tell Hardy she shoot him, and then another of the clients, Deslatte, Moise Deslatte from Maida, he say this Hardy shoot the shotgun too close to him, that the shot hit the blind. On top all that, he claim Hardy, he cheat at cards. They start to fight, but Thiboceaux, he stop them. But not before Deslatte— he be good old boy—but he tell Hardy the same like Cullen do."

"He threatened Hardy?"

"Oui. He do that when Thiboceaux, he be stopping the fight."

"Thiboceaux? Who's he?"

"Louie Thiboceaux. He work for me. He be guide too. Good guide. This Hardy, when Thiboceaux, he stop the fight, Hardy be accusing Thiboceaux that he don't give him good spot to shoot turkey. They argue more. Deslatte, he threaten to shoot Hardy if the man don't leave him alone. Hardy, he want to fight more. That's when I tell Hardy I give his money back, and he leave. Right then."

A small man in jeans and a plaid shirt descended the stairway carrying an armload of dirty linens. Charley brightened up. "There Thiboceaux now. Hey, Thiboceaux. Get yourself over here, *mon*."

Charley introduced us, and the curly-headed man told the same story as Charley.

"And Hardy left that night after the fight, huh?"

A slender, sinewy man, Thiboceaux shook his head. "Not right then. He be too drunk. He decide then he want to fight me." A sneer played over his lips, revealing two missing upper teeth. He grinned at Charley. "That be big mistake, I think."

Charley agreed. "That man, he be drunker than a shrimper on Saturday night, but he do leave before the sun, it come up next morning."

After Thiboceaux disappeared into the bar, I studied the wiry man before me, at the same time thanking my lucky stars that I had decided to come on down to the lodge. More and more loose ends were showing up. I handed him my business card. "There's my cell number, Charley. If you think of anything more about Hardy, I'd appreciate a call."

When I left well after dark, I had a stack of notes that would take me half the night to sort and catalog. While my computer is much faster, I still prefer scribbling notes on the little 3"×5" cards. That way I can mix and match. It is surprising how sometimes by simply putting one card next to another can change the entire complexion of a theory.

By the time I concluded my interview with Charley Benoit, Jack was too drunk to drive. While I had been questioning Charley, Jack had been spiking his drinks with tall tales from the old bartender about loup garous.

By the time I managed to get Jack down to the Cadillac, he had spotted a half–dozen loup garous lurking in the shadows. He stopped at the car door and stared up at me. With affected pomposity, he drew himself upright and announced, "Now that I think about it," he mumbled, slurring his words, "I might be a loup garou, an alcoholic loup garou made this way by a jealous witch." He paused and winked at me. "Whose name we both know, but as a gentleman I decline to speak her name even if she is your ex-wife."

With that, he opened the door and screamed.

"What?" I shouted, startled.

"Look!" He blubbered, pointing to the front seat."

There in the middle of the white leather seat was a muddy human footprint.

"Loup garou! Loup garou!" Jack babbled.

It took me ten minutes and another straight bourbon to coax Jack into the car, but not into the front seat, only the back seat where he promptly passed out.

Charley Benoit shook his head and grinned at Jack. "Kids, I figure. We got some kids around the place. They probably fooling around this big car here while you be inside."

"Loup garou, my eye," I muttered in disgust as we drove away.

Overhead the stars lit the cane on either side of the road with a bluish-silver light, but when we entered the trees, the darkness seemed to press down on us.

I cocked my head, straining to pick up what sounded like the faint sound of metal against metal, but the wind twisting through the feathery cypress leaves played havoc with the sound.

Suddenly, I caught movement through the passenger's side of the windshield. I instinctively slammed on the brakes as a large tree toppled across the road directly in front of us.

Clenching my teeth, I spun the wheel and stood on

the brake pedal, hearing the tires squealing through the roaring in my ears.

From the corner of my eye, I caught movement in the shadows, but when I looked again, all I saw was the forbidding darkness of the swamp.

Chapter Five

That's when the rain began, and by the time Charley Benoit and Louie Thiboceaux cut the tree in two and dragged it off the road with the four-wheel GMC pickup, it was midnight.

We were soaked from the steady rain.

Jack stood silently at my side, sobered by the close call.

Shining a bright halogen beam over the thick trunk of the cypress tree as water dripped from the bill of his cap, Charley muttered, "You be lucky, *mon ami*. This cypress—she fall few seconds later, the car, it and you be flatter that the beaver's tail."

"Maybe luckier than you think," I exclaimed.

"What that you say?"

"Shine the light back to the base of the tree."

The intense beam swept along the fuzzy trunk of the huge cypress, halting at the clean cut at the base. "This sucker didn't fall, it was cut," I muttered, taking the light from his hand and wading into the ankle-deep water. My clothes and shoes were already soaked so a little more water made no difference.

"Cut!" Jack exclaimed. "What do you mean cut?"

I grunted impatiently. "What does anyone mean by cut? Cut! Sliced—as opposed to diced!"

Two-thirds of the base was sliced cleanly. On the perimeter of both the tree and the stump were matching creases in the light-colored flesh of the cypress, indicating that a wedge had been driven into the cut. On the opposite side, a V-shaped wedge had been chopped out of the trunk just below the cut. A professional job.

"See what I mean," I muttered, holding the light on the creases and remembering the faint sound of metal against metal.

"*Mère sainte!* Holy Mother!" Charley exclaimed. "Someone, he don't care none much for you, my friend."

Ignoring his observation, I shined the light into water the color of weak coffee.

"What for you look?"

I grunted with satisfaction and pulled a V-shaped wedge of iron from the water. "This," I replied, holding the wedge for all to see, remembering the movement in the shadows just as the tree fell. "Whoever tried to make us part of the asphalt knew what he was doing. Lucky for us, his timing was off."

Charley muttered in surprise. Jack stuttered, "You mean—you mean, someone tried to kill us? Both of us?"

I nodded, glancing at Thiboceaux who seemed to be bored with it all. "You got another explanation?" I muttered.

On the way into Morgan City, I couldn't help wondering about Thiboceaux. The man didn't seem at all surprised about the obvious attempt on our lives. Of course, to give him his due, Jack and I were strangers, outsiders. We could drop dead in the morning, and it would mean nothing to Louie Thiboceaux or Charley Benoit.

Still I had learned much from Charley and his client records. Sue Cullen owned a small, four-store chain of interior decorators headquartered in Maida with the trendy name Interiors by Suzanne. She and John Hardy checked in at the same time at the lodge, though arriving in separate cars. She was the client to whom Laura Palmo had referred. And she had threatened Hardy.

Then there was Moise Deslatte of Maida, the client with whom Hardy had fought. He also had threatened Hardy. Deslatte owned a construction company. Well known to Charley Benoit, Deslatte was a regular client at the lodge.

I hoped a brief visit with each the next day would provide sufficient information to determine the whereabouts of John Hardy, at least sufficient enough to satisfy his mother.

Unfortunately, the only motel in Morgan City with a vacancy was the Empire Arms Suites, an ostentatious name for a battered row of rooms that appeared to be sagging in every direction. The sleepy clerk informed me there was only a single vacancy, but at one o'clock in the morning, I couldn't afford to be choosy. Luckily, there were two beds, otherwise, I would have slept on the floor.

After depositing my luggage, I went outside for better reception and called Marty's voicemail, making sure he knew where I was. When I went back inside, Jack, fully dressed, had sprawled across one of the beds and was snoring like a chainsaw.

After a quick shower, I climbed between the sheets, which remarkably, were clean. I was asleep as soon as my head hit the thin pillow.

The jangling of my cell phone cut through the deep slumber into which I had fallen. Sleepily, I fumbled on the nightstand for it. "Yeah," I muttered, my eyes still closed.

"Tony. This is Marty. How far are you from Whiskey River?"

I groaned. "Hundred miles or so, I guess."

"Well, you're going to find out." The excitement in his voice cut through the fog in my head. "Just heard from my cousin in Baton Rouge that the sheriff's department in Iberville Parish reported that John Hardy's Suburban has been pulled out of Whiskey River below Interstate 10."

Suddenly, I was wide away. "When?"

"About two o'clock this morning."

I glanced at the clock on the TV. Three thirty-three. *What was the old superstition about threes—bad things happen in threes?* I hoped this wasn't one of them.

Marty continued. "Get over there and find out what's going on. Call me as soon as you hear anything. It looks like this could be more than some rich guy taking off on a lark." What he didn't say was that he was already counting the thirty thousand Josephine Hardy had promised if her son had been harmed.

The rain had eased to a mist.

We packed quickly.

"I'm ready," said Jack, opening the door. "Let's go."

Suddenly he screamed and jumped back into me, knocking me backward. "What the—"

"Snake, snake, snake," he screamed, hiding behind me and pointing at the door.

A startled curse burst from my lips when I saw a four-foot black water snake hanging limply by the tail from the doorjamb. In its mouth was a dead mouse.

Jack was blubbering.

A cold chill ran up my spine. I knew the meaning of the snake and mouse. It was a chilling warning from the old ones to a transgressor, threatening him with the same fate as the mouse, if he continued his pursuit.

Nonsense as far as I was concerned, but despite being several years into the twenty-first century, there were still many believers in gris-gris and wangas out in the swamps; there were still many who were driven by the old superstitions. And as long as they were out there, they had to be taken seriously.

I picked up a chair and poked at the snake. It didn't react. I breathed easier. "It's dead," I muttered, looking again at the mouse in its mouth and remembering Nanna, my great-great grandpa's sister who claimed to be a seer and to whom many had gone for gris-gris and wangas.

"You sure?" Jack had backed up another couple steps.

"Yeah, I'm sure. Come on. Let's go."

"But—"

"Just walk around it, Jack. Come on. Let's get out of here." Grabbing my gear, I scooted around the dangling snake and abruptly jerked to a halt. "Jeez," I muttered.

"What? What?"

"Take a look." I stepped aside and nodded to the Cadillac.

Written on the passenger's window with what appeared to be white shoe polish were the rain-smeared words, "Mind your own business."

Jack cursed. "Look what some yokel did to my Caddie," he shouted, brushing past me.

I grabbed his arm. "Hold on. Look at that." I pointed to the ground beside the car. There in the mud were several footprints, all barefoot, slowly filling with water.

Jack looked around at me, alarmed. "You don't think . . ." He gulped, unable to utter the words stuck in his throat.

I shook my head. "Don't be ridiculous."

"But bare feet. Remember last night at the lodge?" He shook his head. "This is crazy, Tony. This is really crazy."

I remembered. That was the trouble. I remembered too well.

We threw our luggage in the trunk, wiped the words from the window with a threadbare towel, courtesy Empire Arms Suites, and headed for Whiskey River.

I decided against telling Jack the significance of the snake and mouse. He was too jumpy. I didn't believe in all the superstitions, yet he was right about one thing. It was crazy.

Winding, twisting scenic byways don't lend themselves to speed, especially when a fine mist is falling, but we covered the fifty miles of tortuous highway from Morgan City to Lafayette in three quarters of an hour. Then we headed east.

"I said it before, and I'll say it again. These people are weird," Jack muttered, peering into the mist and flexing his fingers about the steering wheel. "A snake. Ugh." He shivered. "What was it, some kind of sign or something?"

I glanced at him, leaned my head back on the seat, and lied. "Beats me."

Jack fell silent, pensive. Several minutes passed. Keeping his eyes on the road, he said. "It's spooky, Tony. If it was the same guy from last night—you know the one who cut the tree down—how did he know where we were?"

All I could do was shrug. That was one question I wished I had the answer for.

At 5:30, in the steady mist, we pulled up in front of the Iberville Parish Sheriff's office in Grosse Tete, French for "big head." I imagine a psychologist could have a field day with the Freudian implications of such a name.

Louisiana law enforcement does not hold Louisiana private investigators in a great deal of esteem, and as far as they're concerned, out-of-state P.I.'s are even lower—on the same level as a cockroach.

So consequently, my faithful fleece-lined leather coat back in Church Point would have provided very little protection from the chilly reception I received from the sheriff's department. I explained Mrs. Hardy's wishes and the details of my visit to their fair state, plus the fact I was a Louisianan first, and a

Texan second, but Watch Sergeant Jimmy LeBlanc shook his head. "We don't need no help over here. We do the job ourselves. We find him. And if something do happen to him, then we handle that too."

Often I think that fortuity is the primary means of most accomplishments. Happenstance sometimes becomes an unexpected but welcome bedfellow, for just before Sergeant LeBlanc dismissed me for Texas, the phone rang. It was from the Opelousas Police Department.

After he replaced the receiver, I commented that I had family in Opelousas, hoping that might make him reconsider. "My cousin. He has a chain of lube shops there. Maybe you've heard of them, Catfish Lube?"

His eyes widened with surprise. "What's that you say? Your cousin, he own Catfish Lube?"

"Yeah."

"You say Leroi Thibodeaux be your cousin?"

I nodded, surprised he knew Leroi.

Recognition lit his eyes, and a broad grin split his dark face, his white teeth a striking contrast against his blue-black skin. "I hear of you. You the white boy that be Leroi's cousin. The one he calls the white sheep in the family."

I grinned. "You know Leroi?"

"Do I? Him and me, we went to LSU together." He shook his head and chuckled. "Me, I could tell you some things about that cousin of yours."

"Not as much as I could tell you," I replied, relaxing.

We exchanged stories about Leroi for a few minutes. I brought the subject back around to the purpose of my visit, explaining my request to inspect the Suburban.

Jimmy LeBlanc hesitated, which gave me the chance to tell him I had information about John Hardy's activities from April 23 through the early morning of the 26. Within a few more minutes, I brought Sergeant LeBlanc up to date on what I had learned from Charley Benoit, and then managed to elicit his permission to inspect the Suburban, which was down at the local salvage yard.

"But yourself, don't you touch nothing, you hear me?" Sergeant LeBlanc cautioned.

"Can I at least look inside? I might get an idea where he is."

His brow furrowed as he pondered my request. Finally, he nodded. "Don't see what that would hurt nothing, and," he added, "you tell us if you find anything."

I offered my hand. "You got it, Jimmy." I scribbled my cell phone number on a piece of paper and handed it to him. "Would you let me know if you find him?"

He grinned amiably. "For Leroi's cousin, I suppose I will."

Barney Knowles owned the salvage yard. I had expected a burley, pot-bellied, cigar-chomping redneck, but Barney was short and lean and dark as swamp water. Pure Cajun without a Cajun name. Go figure.

He eyed me suspiciously and glanced over my shoulder at Jack who was trying to sleep in the front seat. I suggested he call the sheriff's department to confirm my authorization to inspect the vehicle, but he shrugged and nodded to the black Suburban still hooked up to his tow truck. "There she be. Help yourself."

The steady drizzle had carved streaks in the layer of reddish mud that had coated every inch of the Suburban, clogging every crevice, every crease, every curve of the vehicle.

I opened the door of the 2006 Chevrolet Suburban. The smell of fish smacked me in the face. I surveyed the interior. Nothing but pink mud. No luggage, no shotguns, no boots, nothing.

I opened the glove compartment.

More mud and a handful of water-soaked papers.

I eyed the papers hungrily, remembering my promise to Sergeant LeBlanc not to touch anything. I shot a furtive glance at the office, but Barney Knowles was nowhere to be seen.

I retrieved the papers, spread them on the muddy seat and wiped the mud from them. There was an invoice from La Louisanne Import/Export billing Antigua Import/Export for $86,000.00 for Tiki furniture, whatever that was; four or five receipts from the same Shamrock station in Bagotville, the most recent dated April 23, the day Hardy left for the lodge; and the remaining two slips were duplicates of wire transfers from the Bagotville National Bank to the State Bank of St. Kitts and the other to the Dominica Republic Bank.

St. Kitts and Dominica? Geography wasn't my strong suit in high school, but I guessed the two were Caribbean banks. What kind of business was a Louisiana bank doing with offshore banks? I shrugged, figuring that in today's global economy, the smallest bank in Podunk could be doing business with the Bank of Moscow, but to make certain, I copied the account and routing numbers from the duplicates.

From the corner of my eye, I spotted movement at the office. I glanced up to see Barney standing in the door, watching me suspiciously.

I waved, at the same time slipping the papers back in the glove compartment and closing the door. I glanced at the fuel gauge. The needle registered three quarters of a tank. The key was in the ignition. I turned it, but the needle didn't budge.

While I'm no expert on modern technology, I guessed that when the water shorted out the Suburban's computer, the needle froze.

I glanced at the odometer. Only three thousand miles.

Given the size of the gas tanks on Chevrolet Suburban, I guessed a quarter of a tank was about the amount of fuel to cover a hundred miles.

Just before I closed the door, I spotted a matchbook in the mud on the floor. Using the tip of my finger, I brushed the mud from the cover. Bagotville Bank. Must have belonged to Hardy. I eased open the cover. Mud caked the cardboard matches, but not so thick I couldn't see three or four had been plucked from the left side of the matchbook.

Staring off into space, I sorted through what I knew. Hardy left Bagotville on the 23rd; fought with Deslatte on the 25th, called his secretary on the same day telling her he was taking a jaunt to the Bahamas; left the lodge sometime in the early morning hours of the 26th; and on the 27th, called his secretary, Laura Palmo, allegedly from the Bahamas; and today, Friday, April 30th, his vehicle was fished from Whiskey River.

It appeared John Hardy had driven straight to the river without any side trips. The absence of a receipt later than the 23rd, plus three-quarters tank of gas, would indicate such.

Surveying the interior of the vehicle one last time, I studied the layers of mud coating the seats and headliner. I jotted down what I had found on my $3'' \times 5''$ cards before I walked across the lot to Barney Knowles.

"Find what you was looking for?"

I shrugged. "Whatever it was, I didn't see it. Let me ask you a question. You pull many cars out of Whiskey River?"

He pursed his lips. "Some."

"How long you figure that one was in the water? There was a lot of mud in it."

The thin Cajun chuckled. "That old river, she be nothing but mud. Still, I suppose three, four days."

Three or four days.

That little tidbit of information supported my theory that he had driven straight to the river from the lodge, but why?

Chapter Six

The eighteen-mile bridge spanning the Atchafalaya Swamp is actually two bridges separated by a strip of low-lying land a little more than a mile wide, a strip that provides a plethora of convenience stores, liquor stores, beer joints, truck stops, gas stations, and dozens of other small enterprises.

On impulse I pulled off at the small community of Rowan. On either side of the farm road were two convenience stores, Venable's, a thrown-together structure of corrugated iron, clapboard, and plywood, all painted a dark green.

Across the road was a competing convenience store, Kwik Stop, which was in even worse repair. The gasoline lanes were filled with potholes, but the pumps appeared brand new, a concession accorded the business by oil companies anxious to peddle their wares.

Three Harley hogs were parked near the door. In bold Algerian cursive across the gas tank of one were the words Angel of Death.

The inside of Kwik Stop was as shabby as the outside, and from the hallway leading to the restrooms, the cloying odor of unwashed toilets flooded across the racks of produce next to the open doorway.

Jack headed for the men's room while I picked up a couple Nehi crème sodas.

A single biker was making a purchase at the counter, blocking the owner's view of the other two bikers who were openly stuffing various items inside their leather jackets. There was not one of the three I would have cared to meet in a narrow alley on a dark night.

When the three bikers left, I sat the soft drinks on the counter. My experience has been no questions are asked or no restrooms are used unless the customer purchases at least one item.

"Morning," I said to the portly man behind the counter, as I plopped down a twenty.

He snorted at the retreating backs of the bikers. "Be two twenty," he replied by way of greeting.

While he rang up the sale, I pulled out the photo of John Hardy. "Maybe you can help me, friend. By any chance, have you seen this gent the last few days?"

He returned my change, glanced at the photo, and

shook his head. "Them stinking bikers," he growled. "Come in and try to steal me blind."

I shrugged. "Haven't seen him, huh? Maybe three, four days back?"

"Nah. Sure wish they'd find someplace else to camp. They been driving us crazy for the last six months, in and out, in and out." He looked up at me. "Tell me, why don't they go into Baton Rouge instead of coming here. It's just as close."

I was having trouble hanging onto the thread of his conversation, but a couple of his words piqued my curiosity, arousing a crazy idea. "You saying those bozos have been coming in here regular?"

"Too regular. About six months back, forty or fifty set up a camp somewhere on the other side of Whiskey River. Since then, them bikers on the Interstate are thicker than crabs on a dead catfish."

The crazy idea of mine burgeoned into insanity. I jammed the change in my pocket. "Thanks, buddy," I said, glancing around as Jack emerged from the hallway of stench. "Let's go! We got no time to waste!"

Outside, we spotted the bikers heading for the Interstate. "Follow them," I said. "Now! But stay far enough behind they don't notice us."

As we sped along at a steady fifty-five, Jack demanded to know what I had in mind.

"Simple. It's a long shot, but if there are as many bikers motoring up and down the Interstate as our friend back at the convenience store said, then maybe, just maybe one of them saw something when they crossed the bridge over Whiskey River."

Flexing his fingers about the steering wheel, Jack glanced at me, his jowls flopping when he turned his head. "You really think someone saw the Suburban going into the river? That's the craziest idea I ever heard."

I gave him a wry grin. "It's the craziest idea I ever heard too, Jack. Now, just drive."

At the first exit beyond Whiskey River, the bikers turned off. Remaining on the Interstate, we followed from a discreet distance and spotted them turn off the access road onto a narrow dirt lane winding back into the woods.

"Now what?" Jack asked.

"Find me a liquor store."

At Bayou Din Liquors, I bought ten cases of cheap beer and a case of cheaper vodka. "Payoffs," I replied when Jack questioned the purchase. "There's no way I'm walking into the lion's den without enough steak to keep him off me."

"Huh?" Jack frowned. "What are you talking about, steak?"

I rolled my eyes and nodded to the driver's seat. "Just get in and drive, Jack. Head back to where the bikers turned off."

Suddenly, his eyes lit with understanding. "You mean—"

"Yes, Jack. I mean we're going into the bikers' camp."

He gulped hard once or twice, then started the Cadillac.

Thirty minutes later, we pulled off the eastbound Interstate onto the access road, and I instructed him to park just before the dirt lane the bikers had taken.

"Park? I thought we were going to the bikers' camp."

I shook my head. "Not without an invite."

He frowned once again, so I explained, "The old boy back at the convenience store said bikers were all over the Interstate. I plan to stop a couple out here. Show them the booze and offer it to them for answers to a couple questions."

Jack muttered a curse. "They'll cut our throats and leave us out here to the wolves and panthers and whatever else is roaming out here in this forsaken wilderness. I tell you, boy, I'm—"

"Look!" I exclaimed, pointing to the westbound lane, down which two bikers were approaching.

Jack growled. "So what? They're not coming over here. They're heading for Texas."

"There's always the crossover on the other side of the river."

He sneered. "That's going to take almost thirty min—"

Like the good, law-abiding citizens they were, the two bikers had no intention of wasting another thirty minutes. They slowed, cut across the median dividing east- and west-bound traffic, shot over the highway and bounced over the shoulder, and slid to a screeching halt a few feet from the grill of the Cadillac where I had gone to stand when I saw them coming toward us.

They were the archetypal bikers—big, burly, and belligerent. Burgeoning bellies bulging over their belts, they sat on their hogs, glowering at us. The one on the right, his head shaven, and his hairy torso covered by a tank top five sizes too small and covered with holes through which bright red hair curled, unwound a length of chain from his handlebars and climbed lazily off his bike. Gently pounding the length of chain into the palm of a hand that looked the size of a baseball glove, he sauntered toward me. The other, decked out in full leathers, followed.

At that moment, I figured I had made the worst mistake of my life, but there was no turning back. Grendel personified would be on me before I could reach the door, so I gulped and nodded amiably.

"You want something?" He growled, eyeing me malevolently.

Much more casually than I felt, I leaned back against the hood of the Cadillac and folded my arms across my chest and nodded. "Yeah. I do. I want information." His eyes narrowed, and I continued. "And I'm willing to pay." I pushed off the hood and motioned for the two to follow me to the rear of the convertible. "Pop the trunk, Jack."

Jack did, revealing the cases of booze. I gestured to them. "These are yours."

The one in leathers snorted. "What's the catch?"

I held up my hands. "No catch. Just the answer to a couple questions."

"Me and Texas Red here don't answer no questions for nobody." He grinned at his partner. "Do we, Red?"

I glanced at the bright red hair on his torso. At least the moniker was appropriate.

Texas Red eyed the booze and licked his lips. "Depends. What's the question?"

At five-ten, I had to crane my neck to look up at him, and I could see the warning in his eyes. "My name's Tony Boudreaux, Red." I stuck out my hand. For a moment, he hesitated, taken aback by my affable display of friendliness. Finally, he took my hand and grunted. "This here's Pike."

I nodded. "Pike."

Pike nodded, but said nothing. Both of them eyed the booze, then glared at me.

"All I want is for you to ask your friends if any of them happened to see a black Chevrolet Suburban on the levee beneath the Interstate at Whiskey River three or four days ago." I shrugged. "That's it. The booze is yours even if they haven't."

Red and Pike eyed each other. Pike shrugged. "I ain't seen nothing like that, but follow us on back to the digs. You can ask the others." He leaned into the open trunk and tore a bottle of vodka from the case.

He chugged two or three gulps, handed it to Texas Red, and belched. "Let's go."

As he passed Jack, who had remained in the driver's seat, Pike hit him on the shoulder and laughed. "You sure don't say much, little fella, do you?"

We followed the two bikers up the narrow dirt lane that lead back into the thick growth of oak and sweetgum. Jack's normally flushed cheeks were pale as what little snow we get down here in the swamps. "I don't think this is a good idea, Tony. I've seen guys like these back on Sixth Street in Austin. I tell you, they can be animals."

"Keep your eyes on the road and stop worrying. Tell them some of your jokes if you have to. Besides, we're not staying more than a few minutes."

The dirt lane twisted through the dense forest several hundred yards before opening into a clearing the size of a football field. Threatening to collapse at any moment, a ramshackle house sat in the middle of the field with a dozen or so tents of varied colors set up around it and twice as many bikes parked about.

A dozen glowering Neanderthals converged upon us with murder in their eyes and curses rolling off their lips. Right behind them had half as many mamas, muttering scurrilous epithets even more chilling.

Jack whispered. "Tony, I think this is a big, big mistake. They'll bash our heads in, and no one will ever find us."

Texas Red and Pike went to meet them. After a few moments, a nodding of heads and a chorus of cheers told us we would live for another day. Thirty seconds later, all the booze had been shifted to the ramshackle house, and we were dragged along by several laughing, friendly bikers.

Within minutes, everyone had a beer or bottle, even Jack. I held one, but only sipped at it. I'd battled alcohol for years, and this revelry was turning into the kind of party that would make even the most dedicated abstainer swear off A.A.

Unfortunately, no one had spotted a black Suburban on the levee. Jack leaned close and whispered. "Looks like a hundred and fifty bucks down the drain, huh?"

"Afraid so," I mumbled. "You ready to get out of here?"

At that moment, Pike, mellowed out by a bottle of vodka, put his arm around Jack's shoulders and shouted. "This little feller don't say much, boys. We ought to find him some entertainment."

I had no idea what direction the party was about to take, so I hastily spoke up, trying to keep some semblance of control of the situation. "That little feller is a standup comic, Pike. He does an act at the Red Pigeon Nightclub on Sixth Street in Austin."

An overweight mama in full leathers shouted, "Hey, I been there! A real gas, it is. Almost as good as five lines of coke."

Everyone laughed and clamored for Jack to do his

nightclub act, and like all clowns, he agreed, regaling them with a plethora of obscene jokes and stories. There were no aisles to have them rolling in, so they had to settle for the grass. Of course, by this time, so many of them were zonked with the booze and pills that it was impossible to say what put them on the grass, Jack's jokes or the booze.

I couldn't help noticing one of the older mamas was paying special attention to Jack. I didn't think too much about it at the time. When his act was over, I suggested we leave, but to my surprise, Jack backed off. "A few minutes longer," he said, his eyes fixed on the adoring mama. "I'm having a good time. I was wrong. These guys are okay."

Before I could protest, Texas Red waved me over. He pointed to a newcomer, a lanky, heavily bearded biker with suspicious eyes. "This is Demonio, that's Portuguese for the devil, which is what he is when he's mad," he said with a leer. "He saw something."

I forgot all about Jack. I held my breath. "At the river?"

Demonio eyed Texas Red, who shook his head. "No sweat. Tony here's one of us. Don't worry."

Demonio looked at me with eyes cold as ice. "Four or five days ago, I was crossing the river when I spotted a black Chevrolet Suburban parked on the levee. Just before sunup." He paused, then added. "There was a red Jeep parked beside it."

Chapter Seven

I stared at him, not absorbing his words at first. "A red Jeep?"

"Yeah. Looked like a new one. One of them Cherokees."

Before I could question Demonio further, Jack rushed up and grabbed my arm. "Tony. Let's go. You hear? Let's go."

"What's wrong?" I looked around, and standing in the open door of the ramshackle shack was the adoring mama, her hands on her expansive hips and laughing at the top of her lungs.

That was fine with me. I had what I wanted. I turned to Red and extended my hand. "Thanks, Red. Look me up in Austin sometime." I nodded to Demonio. "Thanks."

He grunted. "Where's the booze?"

I pointed to Red. "He'll show you."

Despite my prodding and amusement at Jack's discomfort, he refused to reveal any of the details that prompted him to leave so hastily.

Finally, he jerked his head around and glared at me. "You might as well shut up about it, Tony. You'll never find out what happened back there. Never!"

With a chuckle, I leaned back and closed my eyes.

At noon, Jack pulled up in front of Interiors by Suzanne across the town square from the Cocodrie State Bank in Maida. "Fancy looking place," he commented.

I had to agree. The building was white brick with the name Interiors by Suzanne emblazoned in gold script across windows black as coal. It was bold and striking.

"Back in a few minutes," I said, climbing from the car.

Jack grunted. "I'm going down and pick up some beer and a toothbrush and a change of clothes. I'll be waiting out here for you."

The salesperson directed me to the main office.

Sue Cullen was a petite woman, as striking as the statement her building made to the public. Her ebony black hair fell over her shoulders, a marked contrast to her creamy complexion. Having grown up in the heart of Creole Louisiana, I instantly recognized her genealogy. She wore a subdued, but striking knee-length green skirt and a white blouse with ruffles about the neck and wrists. Her fingernails were at least two inches long, and shaped like green daggers—to match her dress, I guessed.

Sometimes I'm slow on the uptake around women, but it didn't take a brain surgeon to see why Hardy desired an intimate rendezvous with her. I introduced myself.

She smiled brightly. "Private investigator?" She arched an eyebrow. "Hope I haven't done anything wrong."

I laughed. "Nothing like that, Miss Cullen. I—"

"Ms.—" she replied quickly, correcting me. "I haven't been a Miss for several years."

A perfect setup for chivalry. "You couldn't prove it by me, Ms. Cullen."

She laughed, revealing startling white teeth. "My, how gallant. And call me Sue."

I nodded to the north. "I'm Tony, and I grew up over in Church Point. My grandfather Moise taught me manners from the old days."

"I'm grateful to him. There isn't much of that around anymore," she replied, indicating a chair in front of her desk. She fished a pack of Virginia Slim cigarettes from her desk drawer. She held the pack out to me. I shook my head. "You mind if I smoke?"

Those green fingernails of hers fascinated me. "Go right ahead."

After she blew a stream of smoke into the air, she smiled. "Now, how can I help you, Tony?"

"It's about John Hardy. My firm—"

The warm smile on her face froze. Her eyes glinted coldly. The cigarette between her lips trembled. She snapped it from her lips and hissed. "Don't talk to me about that—that—" Then she uttered a couple words you'd never thought would roll off those pristine lips.

I hastened to explain. "My firm has been retained to locate John Hardy. That's all."

A faint smile curled her lips. "Locate? He's missing?"

I nodded.

The smile grew broader. "Personally, I couldn't care any less of the whereabouts of that piece of white trash."

The vehemence in her tone rocked me back in my chair. That must have been some argument they had. I arched an eyebrow and whistled. "I didn't mean to hit a sore spot, Ms. Cullen . . . I mean, Sue. I know you had problems at the lodge, but—"

She glared at me a moment, and then her demeanor softened. "I apologize, Tony. It isn't your fault. It's just that John Hardy—well, he's the most despicable, most reprehensible human being I have ever had the displeasure of knowing."

I gave her a wry grin, hoping to lighten the mood. "Obviously then, John Hardy wouldn't get your vote as Man of the Year."

A glitter of amusement filled her eyes, and she took a long drag from her cigarette. "Obviously," she remarked, punctuating her comment with a stream of smoke. "Maybe Snake of the Year."

"But you were at the lodge together."

"Not together," she replied firmly. "Not the way you think. We met there to discuss business." She hesitated, then explained. "John wanted my company's business. We did over four million last year." With the cigarette firmly entrapped between the slender fingers of her left hand, she gestured to her office. "I have branches in Morgan City, Opelousas, and Lafayette. He learned that I'm an avid hunter, so he invited me on a spring turkey hunt at Benoit's Lodge." She paused, inhaled a lungful of smoke, and then continued, her words rolling off her lips along with the cigarette smoke. "But his idea of a spring turkey hunt included me as the turkey and the hunting blind was his bedroom." She paused, and with a wry grin, chuckled. "I should have known better. John Hardy has the reputation as a womanizer from Morgan City to Lafayette, but I didn't expect him to hit on me." She hesitated, a tiny frown knitting her carefully plucked eyebrows.

"Go on. What else?"

She studied me a few moments longer, then a look of defiance glittered in her eyes. "He threatened to sabotage my business arrangement with the local branch of the Cocodrie State Bank here in town, which he could never do. You see, the president of the Cocodrie State Bank and I were in the same sorority at LSU, so naturally, I was able to work a deal with her to borrow at a much more attractive rate. Have been for years."

I nodded. "Is that when you left?"

Sue's eyes blazed. "As fast as I could, but he grabbed my arm and tried to stop me." A sly smile played over her carefully painted lips. "Being from Church Point, you have an idea of just how enraged a Creole woman can become."

With a knowing grin, I nodded, and she continued. "I was furious. I slapped him as hard as I could." She glared at me defiantly, and then a wry smile curled her lips. "And I didn't even get one free meal out of the whole thing."

With an affable grin on my face, I said, "I heard you threatened to shoot him if he bothered you again."

Her smile froze momentarily, then grew wider. She stared at me levelly. "And I will if he ever comes on to me like he did or tries to ruin my business."

I chuckled. "So then, I don't suppose he has contacted you since that night."

Her eyes narrowed. "If he knows what's good for him, he'd better never contact me again." She laid her hand on her glass-topped desk. I couldn't help noticing the rings on her fingers. On her ring finger was a simple band with tiny diamonds encrusted in it; on her forefinger was another, mounted with a diamond the size of a walnut. "Anything else?"

"Yes. Do you know anyone who drives a red Jeep?"

She arched an eyebrow and stared at me slyly. "A Cherokee?"

I shrugged. "That's what I was told. I don't know the year or the model."

"The only one I know of is a local call girl, Fawn Williams. Her real name is Sophie Mae Brown. That's how she's listed in the directory."

Nodding slowly, I asked one final question. "Did Hardy mention anything to you about a trip to the Bahamas?"

"No."

I rose. "I suppose that's it then. I do appreciate your help."

She smiled warmly. "Good luck. I hope you find him."

I lifted an eyebrow. "From what I've heard about John Hardy, he could be anywhere in the world at this moment."

"As long as he isn't here," she exclaimed, rising and offering me her hand.

Patchy clouds overhead intermittently blocked the blistering rays of the sun. Jack had lowered the top and was sitting behind the wheel with a bottle of Big Easy beer in his hand. He held it up and grinned.

"Bought a case and iced down a half–dozen. Can't get these back in Austin. So, where to now? Home?"

"Nope. Nearest phone carrel."

I got lucky, two ways. The directory had not been torn from the phone carrel, and second, Sophie Mae was listed. But my luck soured when I reached her apartment in the fashionable section of Maida known as Pirates Landing, a development of upscale apartments, only to discover she was not in.

Her apartment was on the third level. The first level provided parking for the tenants. On impulse I had Jack drive through the garage where I spotted a red Jeep Cherokee. "Stop here."

"Huh?"

"Stop! Let me out," I said, climbing from the Cadillac. "Pop the trunk, then drive on out front. I'll be out in a minute."

I fished a slim jim from my bag of tools and ducked between the rows of parked vehicles and waited, studying the shadowy garage. No one was around. Moving stealthily I sidled up to the Cherokee, quickly jimmied the lock, and rummaged through the papers in the glove compartment.

Suddenly I froze, staring at a handwritten receipt for a full tank of fuel from Venable's Convenience Store, dated August 26. Venables! That was the convenience store across the road from the Kwik Stop where I had latched on to the bikers.

I jammed the receipt in my pocket, glanced around the dark garage furtively, then stuffed the other papers back in the glove compartment.

Two minutes later I climbed into the Cadillac and nodded at Jack.

With a deep sigh, he asked, "Where to now?"

"North."

An hour later, we pulled into Venable's Convenience Store, and I went inside. A wizened little man with a shiny bald head stood behind the counter, a half-smoked cigarette clutched between his bony fingers. I glanced around. I was the only customer.

He nodded. "What'll you have?"

"A couple questions, if you don't mind." I handed him the snapshot of Hardy. "Have you seen this guy around?"

For a moment, he eyed me suspiciously, then shook his head. I then unfolded the receipt and handed it to him. "Did you write this?"

He didn't move. "You the law?"

I shook my head. "Just a guy trying to find a guy." I offered him the receipt again.

He studied it a moment, then shook his head. "Nope."

His response took me aback momentarily. "Could someone else have written it?"

The shriveled old man studied it a few more seconds. "That looks like Baptiste's writing." He nodded. "Yep. I say that's Baptiste writing."

"Is he around?"

His eyes narrowed. "You say you ain't the law?"

"No, I'm not the law."

He shrugged. "Jean Baptiste, he be in the back, peeling shrimps."

If possible, Jean Baptiste was even more wrinkled, more shriveled than old Venable, but his bony fingers were a blur as he peeled and deveined shrimp. With a cigarette dangling from his lips, he glanced at the receipt as he grabbed another shrimp. "You bet, that be my writing. Crazy woman—she don't pay by the credit card. She pay cash, and then insist on the receipt, she." He popped the vein from the spine of the shrimp and grabbed another crustacean. Wielding the plastic deveiner, he shoved it under the shell and into the intestinal canal of the shrimp, removing the waste and shell in one deft move.

"Can you describe her?"

A leering grin split his corrugated face. He squinted through the cigarette smoke and his cigarette waggled up and down as he replied. "You bet. She be a looker, but don't go telling my old woman I said that. This one, she gots red hair." He chuckled and nodded to the receipt. "This woman, she be a real looker." He emphasized his comments by using the deveiner to exaggerate the outline of her curves in the air.

"What about her skin? Dark? Light?"

He pursed his lips and concentrated. "Hard to say.

She wear sunglasses and one of them scarves over her head, but it look kind of halfway betwixt. Kinda dusty-like."

I thanked him and left. Now all I had to do was meet Fawn Williams and see if "she gots red hair" and the shapely curves the old man outlined.

"Now where?" Jack asked when I climbed back in the car.

"Back the way we came."

A disappointed frown wrinkled his forehead. "Back to Bagotville?"

I sensed the reluctance in his tone. I nodded. "Yeah, I want to see a man about a card game."

Chapter Eight

Traffic was light on Highway 90, a welcome relief from the congestion on I-10 and the tortuous curves on the Scenic Byway. In Bagotville, I planned a brief visit with Moise Deslatte, and then another one with Laura Palmo, before driving on down to Maida and hoping to finally visit Fawn Williams.

More and more I was coming to believe that if John Hardy had taken a trip, it was one that someone else had planned for him, and in all probability one he would not have chosen for himself.

Thirty minutes later we pulled up in front of Deslatte Construction, but Moise Deslatte was at his fishing camp back in the swamps of Bayou Teche. I smiled at his secretary and promptly lied. "He mentioned something about a fishing camp when we were hunting turkeys a few days ago down at Benoit's Lodge."

She lifted an eyebrow. "Oh, you be down at the camp too, huh?"

A private investigator is often called upon to think fast, lie easily, and play innocent. Not to brag, but I lie and feign innocence with a certain degree of what I consider skilled accomplishment. However, there are those who question my ability to think fast. This time I fooled them.

Figuring he had told her of his confrontation with Hardy, I replied, "Yeah. I was at the table when that jerk, Hardy, tried to cheat your boss."

That was all it took to sell my credibility. Within minutes, I had the location of Deslatte's fishing camp and a veiled suggestion of a clandestine date that night, which I declined.

When we parked in front of Mae's Boat and Bait Camp, Jack raised the top and turned on the air conditioning. "You go on. I'm going to stay here where it's cool."

"You sure?"

"I'm sure. How long will it take?"

I nodded to the aluminum rental boats pulled up on the shore. "An hour, more or less. If—," I added, "I got the directions right."

Sweat rolled down his plump cheeks that were rosy red from the heat. "I'll wait," he replied, patting the steering wheel.

"Whatever." I headed for the office at the same time two bearded, gap-toothed swamp rats ran up on the sandy shore in an aluminum jon boat with the motor wide open, the accepted method of docking a small boat in the swamps.

By the time I reached the office, the heat and humidity had my shirt clinging to my skin. Inside, ignoring my A.A. pledge, I picked up a cold six-pack of beer to ward off the heat, rented a boat, and checked my directions to the camp.

"Moise, he still be at the camp," the old Cajun proprietor said, pointing to an empty slip in the boat basin. "That be where he dock his boat."

Leaving the office, I met the two swamp rats coming in. I nodded, making only brief eye contact. The first one ignored me, but the second snarled.

Growing up, I'd seen and known men like them, living back in the swamps, heeding only those rules they made for themselves. Life deep in the Louisiana swamps is a whole different world, unaffected by the pressure and technology of the modern world, nor governed by its laws.

I frowned when I saw Jack standing by the rental boats instead of sitting in the air-conditioned car. "I'm going with you," he said in a rush.

"I thought you were staying in the air conditioning."

He glanced at the office. "Did you see those two?"

"Yeah. What about them?"

He gulped, and I would have sworn even more sweat popped out on his forehead and rolled down his flushed cheeks. "They stopped and looked at me and the car. I think one of them was even drooling." He shook his head. "No way I'm staying around here with those two."

I couldn't keep from laughing.

Jack glowered. "It isn't funny. They look like those retards straight out of that old movie, *Deliverance!*"

Holding up the six-pack, I laughed again. "All right. Since you're going with me, get the ice chest."

Two minutes later, with me in the stern and Jack in the bow to balance the fourteen-foot jon boat powered by a ten horsepower Johnson, we headed back into the swamp, following a twisting bayou. Along the bayou, I spotted several small canals, oil company excavations for pipelines, which formed a spiderweb of narrow waterways through the low-lying ground. Finally, we emerged from the cypress swamp into an ocean of sea cane.

The sun beat down, baking our shoulders. I gulped my beer in an effort to slake my thirst. The wall of cane on either side slid by as we left the brown swamp water behind and skimmed over the clear green water of the fresh tributaries emptying into the swamp.

"How much longer?" Jack demanded, looking back at me, his rotund face beet red from the unrelenting sun baking our head and shoulders and heating the skin of the aluminum boat.

"Any time now if I followed the directions right." And sure enough, around the next bend, we spotted a ramshackle row of tottering cabins with adjoining porches floating on the water in front of the cane. Two jon boats and a open-bow tri-hull were tied to the porches.

At the end of the cabins, two men, who could have been twins of the two back at the bait camp, stood on the porch, tugging on a rope stretched taut. Water exploded at the end of the rope, and I instantly cut off the throttle and drifted to a halt twenty or thirty yards out.

We watched as the two hauled in a six-foot alligator. As the twisting, spinning alligator drew near the porch, one of the men grabbed a lever action rifle and shot into the churning water. Almost instantly, the water grew calm.

Jack looked around at me in amazement.

I shrugged. "Welcome to Louisiana 'gator hunting."

We waited until they dragged the alligator up on the porch and turned their attention to us.

I held up a hand. "Mr. Deslatte?"

The two looked at each other, then one stuck his head inside an open door. Moments later, a short man with a waistline that would match Jack's, stepped outside. The porch seemed to sink another few inches into the water. "Yeah? What you want?"

I gestured to the cabins. "Can we come aboard?"

The roly-poly man studied us a moment, then waved us in.

"Throw me your line," one of the men yelled. He grabbed it and quickly wrapped it around a cleat at the edge of the porch.

Jack remained in the bow of the jon boat as I climbed out and offered Deslatte my hand and introduced Jack and myself. With a wary glance over my shoulder at the dead alligator on the porch, I explained that I was trying to locate John Hardy.

Before I could utter another word, he exclaimed, "That one, he be a lying cheat. He be no good, and I don't want to hear that one's name, you hear?"

"I don't blame you. I heard what took place. I'd get mad too if someone fired off a shotgun in my direction or tried to cheat me," I replied, referring to the incidents at the turkey blinds. That little tidbit of empathy seemed to mollify him, at least for the moment.

He shook his head. "That one, he be crazy. Always has been."

"I know. Did you just meet him at the lodge?"

"On, mais no. Him, I be knowing for—" He paused, shrugged, "'bout twelve, thirteen year now, ever since he come to Bagotville. My company, it done business with his bank. He give good rates, better than the bank in Maida, but no more. Me, I be around here all my life. I ain't never seen a no-good like that one."

I glanced at his two friends who were standing behind the shorter man, staring at me with eyes devoid of emotion. "Look, Mr. Deslatte. John Hardy is missing. Early this morning, the Iberville Sheriff's Department pulled Hardy's Chevrolet suburban from Whiskey River." I paused to give my words time to sink in, then continued, "I've no hard proof, but it looks like he's dead."

Deslatte's eyes grew wide, then narrowed warily. "You think I kill him?"

"No." I shook my head, figuring now was neither the time nor place to be absolutely truthful. A man, any man, can disappear in a heartbeat in Louisiana swamps. "I'm wondering if you know of any enemies he might have had or if he said anything to suggest he had plans other than to go back to work when the hunt was over."

For the first time, his two friends laughed.

One elbowed the other. "You hear that, Juju?"

Juju shook his head. "Do the man have enemies? Do the 'gators got teeths? That best laugh I got me all week, Marcel."

Moise Deslatte winked at me. "What do that say to you?"

I grinned at him. "Will you tell me who they are?"

He hesitated, a frown darkening his rotund face. "How you be finding me out here?"

My grin grew wider. "Why, I told you, Mr. Deslatte. I'm a private investigator. I find people."

He considered my answer a moment, then roared. "Yeah, but you ain't found Hardy."

We all laughed at my expense.

"So, can you help me?"

Amiably he nodded. "Oui. What you want to know?"

"I know Hardy left the lodge early the next morning. How long did you stay?"

"The trip, it be over yesterday. I go by my office and tell my secretary I be here."

"What about his enemies? From the way you laughed, he must have them."

He gave me a crooked grin. "Where do I start? How about with the ex-wife, Janelle Bourgeois. He dump her years ago. Last I hear, she be waitin' tables up in Mowata."

"Mowata? That's back west of Branch, isn't it?" I asked, trying to place the small Louisiana hamlets.

"That be right. North of Rayne. You know the saying, north of Rayne is Branch, and if that ain't wet enough for you, west of Branch is Mowata."

We all laughed. I glanced at Jack who wore a puzzled expression.

I jotted Janelle Bourgeois' name on a 3" × 5" card. "You know what restaurant?"

"Naw. There be only one café in Mowata. That be about the only thing in Mowata," he added with a grin.

"What do you know about her? Anything?"

He laughed. "Me, I knows that one all my life. We was *enfants,* children down to Maida." He shook his head and chuckled. "She always be having the temper, *moyen,* mean temper, even in the school with the sisters."

"Sisters?"

"Oui. The nuns."

I nodded. "Anyone else?"

Deslatte chewed on his bottom lip. "Let's see. There's the gambler, Jimmy Blue, there in Maida at the Louisianne Casino. And then there's the ones who lost all their money when his first bank went under."

"When was that?"

He arched an eyebrow. "Let's see. That be fifteen, maybe twenty years ago. Big scandal up in Opelousas."

"Scandal? You mean the bank going bust?"

"That, and before. His first partner, let's see—" He scratched his bald head. "Babin, that was his name. Duclize Babin. He shoot hisself in the head, they say. Then a few years later, Babin's wife, she be convicted of embezzling money from the bank. She go to state prison. And then, not long after, the bank, it fold up." He shook his head regretfully. "I know that woman all her life. Go figure. You know?"

I nodded thoughtfully. "What was her given name?"

Without hesitation, Deslatte replied. "It be Karen. Karen Babin."

"She must be out of prison by now."

Juju tapped Deslatte on the shoulder and whispered in his ear. The rotund man grunted. "Juju, he say Babin's wife killed in car wreck. Burned to crisp."

Marcel sneered. "That a lot to burn. She big woman, maybe two hundred pounds, I say. Look like beer keg. Every time I see her up in Opelousas, her blond hair is tied up on top of her head." He made the shape of a bouffant over his head. He snorted. "Bet that woman don't have no hair like that in prison."

"Oui!" Juju sneered. "When her crazy brother, that Thertule, he hear she be dead, he run off into the swamps. Ain't nobody seen him since. He crazy. I always figured she be crazy too, her."

Deslatte laughed. "At least half crazy. Thertule, he be a Pellerin, her half brother."

Juju grew serious. "They say the cauchemar, she done makes Thertule a loup garou."

I wanted to laugh, but from the earnest concern on Juju's face, I knew he was deadly serious. I would get nowhere tromping on another's beliefs, regardless how outrageous. Behind me I heard Jack cough.

Deslatte grinned crookedly. "Me, I don't know about that, but it don't bother me none if the man be dead. I don't do it because that one, he ain't worth it."

"What's with him and Jimmy Blue at the casino. Gambling?"

The smile vanished from Deslatte's plump face. "I hear that." His voice grew soft, almost conspiratorial. "I don't know for sure, but me, I hear that them two, they sometimes have business deals." He shrugged and held his hands out to his side. "That I hear. Me, I don't know nothing for certain."

Marcel's shout interrupted us. "Look there. There be a big one."

Floating just below the surface of the calm water thirty feet out was another alligator, his eyes and tip of his snout barely breaking the calm water.

I guessed this one was about eight feet, judging by the distance from the eyes to the snout, which was about two feet.

Juju ducked inside and returned with another rope and a large hook on the end. "Where be the bait?" he whispered urgently.

Marcel opened a box. "There ain't none."

Juju cursed. "We need bait. That a big one out there."

Marcel's eyes lit up. "The cat. We'll use the cat." He popped inside the cabin and returned with a white kitten that couldn't have been more than six or eight weeks old.

Just as he handed the kitten to Juju, I laid my hand on his arm. "Wait."

The two of them looked around at me. From the chilling expression in their eyes, I had the feeling they would just as soon use me for bait as the kitten. "Not the kitten," I said.

Juju snorted. His brows knit in anger. "It ain't none of your business. He ain't no good. Besides, he's all we got left."

"I'll pay you for him. Fifty bucks?"

Marcel muttered a curse. "You crazy. That cat ain't worth fifty bucks."

"It is to me."

Deslatte spoke up. "The 'gator's worth more den fifty dollars."

"How much? Name it."

After some haggling, we settled on two hundred.

Any goodwill I had built with Juju and Marcel had vaporized when I interfered with their alligator fishing. I paid them, handed the kitten to Jack, and climbed back in the jon boat.

I glanced at my watch as we pulled away from the fishing camp. Six-thirty. I rolled my shoulders. It seemed as if two months had passed since Marty's call about the Suburban had jerked me from a sound sleep at 3:33 that morning.

I was exhausted, and the steady drone of the small motor and the sun baking my shoulders combined to lull me into a state of drowsiness. The day had been long and hard, and as we sped back toward the bait camp with Jack holding the kitten, I was looking forward to a hot shower, a good meal, and a clean bed.

Jack spoke up. "Hey, Tony, that guy talked about

one of those loup garous you told me about. Was he serious?"

I nodded. "There's still a lot of superstition out here in the swamps. Nothing to it though."

Before Jack could reply, the guttural roar of a powerful motor ripped through the still air, and a deep-V powerboat with two men behind the console burst through the wall of sea cane, heading directly toward us with every intention of slicing our small boat into two pieces.

Chapter Nine

"Tony!" Jack screamed.

I ignored his shouts. Twisting the throttle to full power, I cut toward the cane, angling away from the powerful boat roaring across the water on a collision course with us. I glanced to my right, grimacing when I saw that the driver had altered his course in an effort to cut me off before I could reach the sea of cane.

Our little jon boat couldn't outrun the big deep-V. Our only chance was to outmaneuver him. Jack shouted above the roar of the motors. "He's going to hit us, Tony! Turn this thing."

When the wicked bow of the speeding boat was almost upon us, I whipped the small aluminum boat to the left, almost pivoting on the stern and heading back in the opposite direction. A cold chill swept over me despite the suffocating heat when I glimpsed the men behind the console as the boat shot past. They were the two swamp rats from Mae's Fish and Bait Camp. Their wake almost swamped us.

The racing powerboat made a broad circle, and by the time he completed the circle, we had reached the cane and were racing through it, running over the slender stalks. Jack sat hunched in the bow, frozen with fear and clutching the kitten to his chest. Deep in the cane, I cut back in the direction of the bait camp, hoping that in our blind rush through the cane, we would not run aground.

Off to the right came the sound of our pursuit slamming into the cane. Moments later, the powerboat shot past our stern, missing us by about ten yards. Instantly the driver whipped in a circle. I cut to the right, and shot into the open water.

Then I spotted one of the oil line canals, a narrow waterway less than five feet wide and lined with thick growth of underbrush hanging over the edge of the water. I cut sharply toward it.

I threw a hasty glance over my shoulder. The powerboat leaped from the cane. Jack's eyes were wide. His mouth was working, but the combined roar of the motors drowned his words.

The pitch of the powerful motor intensified into a shrieking whine. The boat barreled down on us. Our little ten horsepower engine strained. It seemed as if we were standing still. Slowly, the mouth of the canal grew closer.

By now the screaming powerboat was less than thirty yards behind us. I clenched my teeth, straining every muscle to urge our little boat to move faster.

"Hurry, Tony, hurry!" Jack shouted, clutching the tiny kitten to his chest.

The next instant, we shot into the canal. The square bow slammed the underbrush aside. Branches snapped and leaves flew. I glanced over my shoulder, expecting our pursuer to swerve, but he had not altered his course.

He hit the mouth of the small canal, and when he did, the sharp bow of the large boat shot out of the water. All I saw next was a white blur as the powerboat bounced over the canal levee and slammed into the thick undergrowth beyond.

I slowed the jon boat, and that's when Jack screamed and started kicking at the deck. "Snake, snake, snake." At his feet, a yellow and black water snake slithered rapidly across the deck and gracefully arched over the gunnel into the water.

Jack sighed with relief, then cursed at the top of his lungs. "Snakes! They're everywhere!"

And then I caught the musky smell of snake. I looked forward. Stretched on the branches reaching out over the canal lay hundreds of sunning snakes, mostly small because, fortunately for us, the slender branches could not support the heft of larger snakes. "Stay in the middle of the boat, Jack!" I shouted above the purring on the engine. "They're more scared of you than you are of them."

He snorted. "You want to bet?" I didn't think his face could grow any whiter than it was, but it paled noticeably when he gagged and jabbed his arm at the levee ahead. "Stop this thing, Tony. There's an alligator."

I couldn't stop unless I wanted the sunning snakes to start dropping in the boat. Perched on the levee within spitting distance was the alligator, a small one, maybe five feet, but large enough to create panic if he launched himself into the jon boat as it passed. Those black, beady pupils in those yellowish-green eyes watched us. "Just be quiet, Jack. He won't bother us."

"H . . . How do you know that?"

"I just know," I lied, mentally crossing my fingers.

We both sighed with relief after we shot past the alligator. Now all we had to worry about were the snakes. Two or three more fell into the boat but quickly slithered over the side.

Five minutes later, we emerged back into the cypress swamp and headed for the bait camp. By now the sun was dropping below the treetops. The shadows were creeping over the swamp, and we were limp with relief.

Finally, we scraped ashore. Jack climbed out and,

breaking into a string of profanity, staggered toward his Cadillac, which sat forlornly on four flat tires.

By the time road service drove out from Maida and changed four tires, the moon was high in the sky, and the mosquitoes were doing their best to either drain our blood or carry us off.

During the drive into town, I called Charley Benoit and asked if Moise Deslatte had left the lodge on the night Hardy vanished.

"Mais no. The man, he be so mad, he keep the bar open all night."

I thanked him and punched off. Jack glanced at me. The headlights from oncoming cars lit the fear on his face. "Don't lie to me, Tony. Who's trying to run us off? Deslatte?"

"He wouldn't have had the time. None of them—Deslatte, Juju, or Marcel—were ever out of our sight. Then ten minutes after we leave, that boat jumps us. Those two were waiting for us."

"What two?" He frowned at me.

"The two back at the bait camp. You remember, the two who were eyeing this car."

Jack gulped. "You sure?"

"Positive. Now, the big question. Just how did they know we were going to go out there?"

"They saw us at the bait camp."

"No. What I mean is, how did they know we were at the bait camp?"

He flexed his fingers about the steering wheel and pursed his lips. "It's spooky, Tony. I know you say there's nothing to that loupy garou business, but how does whoever it is know where we are all the time. I tell you, it's almost supernatural."

I knew how he felt even though I also believed there was a logical explanation for the series of eerie events. "It isn't supernatural. Someone is behind it."

"Then who?"

I shook my head slowly. "Who have we talked to? Laura Palmo, Hardy's personal secretary; Charley Benoit; Sue Cullen." I paused, and with a chuckle added, "Your biker friends."

"Don't go there, Tony."

I laughed again. "And Sergeant Jimmy LeBlanc and Deslatte's secretary."

Jack shook his head, his heavy jowls flopping. "It just doesn't make sense to me."

Nor did it to me.

But one fact stuck in my head, one indisputable, incontestable fact that made my blood boil. Someone was trying to scare us off, not once or twice, but four times: the falling tree, the dangling snake, the message on Jack's Cadillac, and now, the powerboat.

And if they were that determined to frighten us off, then there had to be more to the case than simply a man dropping out of sight.

Chapter Ten

W e stopped at the first motel we came to, The Cypress Knee, which obviously took its name from the swamp behind it filled with cypress knees protruding from the dark water.

By no stretch of the imagination could I be called a stickler for detail, but usually when I'm working a case, each evening, I'll routinely plan the next day's itinerary.

However, after the harrowing day Jack and I had just survived, and despite the anger surging through my veins, I didn't even take time to undress before hitting the bed, nor even exert the effort to shove the kitten off the pillow where he had decided to sleep next to my head.

The last thing I remember was Jack had plopped

down on his mattress and had pulled a bottle of beer out of the case he had placed by the side of his bed.

During the night, I felt the tiny kitten suddenly bounce off the pillow, and moments later, I heard her tiny paws hit the floor. Then she hissed and yowled. A warning screamed in my numbed brain. I jerked upright and fumbled for the lamp on the nightstand next to the bed.

Snapping it on, I spotted the kitten in the middle of the floor, back hiked, hackles quivering, and facing the spade-shaped head and black coils of a cottonmouth water moccasin.

Instantly, I was wide awake, my frantic eyes darting about the room for a weapon, anything I could use.

From the other bed, Jack mumbled, "Hey, what's going on?"

I shouted over my shoulder. "Stay on the bed, Jack. A snake's in here."

Jack screamed and began shouting some of the most creative profanity I'd ever heard. In the next instant, some sort of missile flew past my head and slammed into the floor in front of the coiled snake.

I jerked around to see Jack, looking like a bowling ball wearing boxer shorts and undershirt bouncing up and down on the mattress, grab another bottle of beer from the case beside his bed and hurl it at the snake, all the while screaming and shouting. The glass bottle shattered in front of the cottonmouth, showering the serpent with Big Easy beer and glass.

When the first bottle exploded in front of the snake, the tiny kitten jumped aside, startled, but quickly returned to the attack, hissing and snarling and lashing out at the weaving head of the cottonmouth.

The combination of exploding beer bottles and a yowling kitten must have unnerved the cottonmouth, for abruptly, the serpent slid sinuously out of his coil and slithered across the floor, disappearing through the narrow crack between the open door and the jamb.

Jack unleashed a final bottle that burst just behind the retreating snake.

And then all fell silent until the motel patrons on either side of us pounded on the wall, and in less than polite terms, shouted for us to be quiet.

We stared at each other for several moments. I tried to still the pounding of my heart and sort the confusion of thoughts running through my head. "You came in after I did, Jack. Are you sure you closed the door?" I hoped he hadn't. If he had, then that could mean only one thing.

In a shaky voice, he replied, "I think so. I'm not certain. I was worn out, but I'd swear I closed it."

Slipping into our shoes, and armed with bottles of beer, we searched the room. To my relief, we found no snakes under the beds or curled in the corners. When we completed our search, Jack and I looked at each other and nodded.

Without a word, we dressed, packed, loaded up, and the three of us—Jack, me, and the little kitten—found ourselves another motel for what little remained of the night.

When I awakened next morning, the tiny kitten was sleeping on the pillow beside me. I couldn't help grinning. I hadn't wanted another pet, not after Oscar, my little Albino Barb exotic fish, died, and my cat, Cat, vanished. On the other hand, I couldn't let Marcel and Juju use the kitten for alligator bait, and I couldn't dump him alongside the road, and now the little guy had perhaps saved our lives.

So with a sigh of resignation, I knew that in the grand scheme of things, I was stuck with another pet. And if the truth were to be known, I'm better with pets than with people, having been divorced once and then in an on-again, off-again relationship for the last several years with Janice Coffman-Morrison, heiress to one of the largest distillery fortunes in the state of Texas and my one-time partner in the detective business.

I rolled over, and, stretching, felt like I was caked with an inch of dirt, but before I climbed out of bed, I quickly scanned the floor. With a sigh of relief, I padded into the bathroom.

After a hot shower, shave, and other morning amenities, I slipped into clean jeans and a Polo shirt. I felt human once again.

I wadded my soiled clothes into a plastic bag. I hesitated, staring at the kitten sleeping peacefully on my pillow. I put the rest of Jack's beer in the ice chest and rolled off some tissue paper to spread in the bottom of the box for the kitten. I'd have to pick up a carrier and litter box later.

We decided to visit the local IHOP for breakfast, and over a rib-sticking meal of fried eggs, pancakes, spicy sausage, grits, gravy, biscuits, and hot coffee, Jack brought up the snake in our room. "Someone doesn't want us around here, Tony. You know that?"

I grinned crookedly. "Oh, really? Now what makes you think that, Jack?"

He arched an eyebrow. "Don't get funny. Look, I know I closed the door. I've been thinking about it. I remember because I automatically reached up to lock the safety chain and there wasn't one. That's how I remember. Someone turned that snake loose in our room, maybe the same someone who tried to run us down with the boat. Or the tree," he added. His face grew serious, and he leaned over the table.

"How did they know where we were, Tony? What have we got ourselves into?"

"I don't know. For whatever reason, someone is trying to scare us off."

"Why?"

With a sigh, I shrugged and popped a chunk of pancake drenched with butter and pecan syrup in my mouth. "I've thought about that. I've got a couple ideas, but nothing definite. One thing is certain," I added, jabbing my fork at him for emphasis, "we're going to find out."

With a resigned shake of his head, he scooped up some grits and gravy. "I hope you're right," he muttered. I could tell from the expression on his face that he wasn't convinced.

Throughout the remainder of the meal, I tried to formulate the questions for Laura Palmo.

Had she heard from John Hardy; had she told anyone of my visit with her; what did she know about Hardy's gambling or his dealings with Jimmy Blue; what was the relationship between Hardy and his ex-wife, Janelle Bourgeois; did she know anything about Fawn Williams; had she heard Hardy even mention the name Babin; and who might be around to tell me of Hardy's defunct bank back in the eighties?

After interviewing Palmo, I planned to visit Fawn Williams and see what explanation she had to offer about the gas receipt from Venable's Convenience Store on April 26th. And, not knowing when I'd get back to Austin, I decided to see if I could talk Sue Cullen into keeping my kitten until I found John Hardy.

From there, it was a lengthy trip up to Mowata and Hardy's ex-wife, Janelle Bourgeois.

Outside the restaurant, Jack and I paused, enjoying the sun and reveling in the sinful meal we had just devoured. He patted his ample stomach. "I wish I could have kept on eating," he remarked with a grin.

"Yep. I was hungrier than I thought." I held up a link of sausage wrapped in a napkin. "I imagine the kitten is too."

Jack grew serious. "Tony, about yesterday and last night. What you said back in there. Do you really think that all they're trying to do is scare us?"

I understood the question he had not asked. "I hope so."

Before he could reply, my cell phone rang. It was Sergeant Jimmy LeBlanc. "Tony? We think we done found John Hardy."

I frowned at his choice of words. "Think?"

"Yeah," he replied with a chuckle. "Hard to tell for sure. He's not all here."

"I don't understand, Jimmy. What do you mean, he isn't all there?"

"He be some dissolved up. A hunter cut open the belly of a big 'gator, and there Hardy be, him!"

The unexpected announcement set me back on my heels momentarily. I collected my thoughts and grimaced at such a gruesome, painful death. "What makes you think it might be Hardy?"

"They find diamond ring in the 'gator's belly with initials J.H. on the inside. The coroner's coming out, he. They always do autopsies in Lafayette."

"Can I see the body there?"

"Sure. I be sure to tell coroner. But—" he hesitated.

"But what?"

"But that not the only thing that be odd about all this."

I arched a quizzical eyebrow at Jack. "You lost me on that, Jimmy. What do you mean not the only thing odd?"

His voice had a puzzled tone to it. "The body, it not be at Whiskey River where the suburban was found."

"No? Where did they find it?"

"You not going to believe me, Tony, but the 'gator what eat him, they killed on Bayou Teche down between Maida and Bagotville in Terrechoisie Parish, not up in the Atchafalaya Basin near Whiskey River."

My jaw must have hit my feet because Jack looked up at me in surprise. "What the? Tony, what's wrong?"

I waved for Jack to button his lip. I stammered a moment. "You . . . you . . . ah . . ." Finally, I managed to form intelligible sounds. "How do you explain that, Jimmy? I mean, eighty to a hundred miles away."

"Me, I don't know how to explain it. All I know is that the sheriff boys in Terrechoisie Parish call me about the body and the ring."

Finally, I managed to collect my thoughts. "What time you figure they'll have the body in Lafayette?"

"Sometime after dinner. This is Sunday. The coroner, he probably going to want to eat hisself a big Sunday dinner of stuffed pork chops, *maque choux,* and rice."

"All right. I'll talk to you later."

I punched off. Now I had one more question for Laura Palmo.

Jack frowned up at me when I dropped the phone back in my pocket. "What was that all about?"

I told him, and for a moment, I thought that huge breakfast of his might come back up.

Being a Sunday, the bank was closed, but Laura Palmo graciously consented to see me at her home. After we checked out of the motel and stopped by a local Walmart to pick up a cat carrier and nuggets for the kitten, we headed toward Bayou Teche.

My thoughts drifted.

If the dead man was John Hardy, then that meant he was probably murdered just after he left Benoit's Hunting Lodge, and the killer drove his Suburban a hundred miles to Whiskey River. That also indicated that there were at least two involved.

Jack broke into my thoughts. "Something wrong?"

"Huh? Oh, no. Nothing. Just thinking."

"Here we are," he announced.

"Huh?" His words jerked me back to the present.

"We're here. That secretary's place."

It was like a scene from a movie.

A white Pontiac sat in the garage of a neat brick home overlooking the bayou. Giant live oaks surrounded the well-maintained two-acre grounds, and the warm honeysuckle breeze swayed the long strands of Spanish moss dangling from the limbs.

Laura Palmo smiled warmly when she opened the door. "Come in, please. You're lucky. I went to early mass today." She paused when she spotted Jack in the Cadillac. "Your friend can come in if he wishes."

"No, thanks. He prefers sitting out there with a bottle of beer and listening to the birds."

"Kind of early, isn't it?"

"You don't know Jack. He loves birds," I shot back.

She laughed. "I wasn't talking about the birds," she said as she led me through a tastefully, but modestly decorated living room and dining room onto the sun porch overlooking the bayou. "This is much more comfortable," she announced, indicating a chaise lounge with gaily flowered cushions. She sat on the edge of a couch, ankles together and her slender hands folded on her knees.

Despite the heat, she wore long sleeves and slacks. "Mr. Hardy hasn't returned yet if that's what you're wondering. Maybe he'll come in sometime today. He must be having fun in the Bahamas."

I arched an eyebrow. "You haven't tried to contact him?"

She shivered. "Heavens, no. Didn't I tell you? He'd probably fire me if I did. He told me to call only in an emergency."

"But what about business? What if something comes up that needs his attention?"

Her black eyes smiled. I sensed a hint of resentment in her tone when she replied, "Marvin Gates takes care of everything. Gates and Mr. Hardy are partners. When I told him about Mrs. Hardy hiring you to find her son, he just laughed and said the same thing I told you—that John pulls this trick all the time."

I hesitated, cataloging the fact she had told Marvin Gates about my job. I debated whether to tell her about Jimmy LeBlanc's call. "Did John Hardy wear a diamond ring?"

A puzzled frown wrinkled her forehead. "Why, yes." She touched a manicured finger to the diamond ring on her right hand. "Silver gold. Three one-carat diamonds in a cluster."

"With his initials inside?"

She nodded, her face reflecting her confusion. A look of alarm filled her eyes. "Has something happened to Mr. Hardy?"

"I don't know. His Suburban was found in Whiskey River yesterday morning. This morning, the Iberville Sheriff's department called me. They found a body." I deliberately shirted any details concerning the location of the body or method of death. "There's no positive identification, not yet. They did find a diamond ring with the initials J.H. The Lafayette coroner will do an autopsy. We'll know then for sure later today."

She pressed her hand to her lips, her composure starting to crumble. "But, it couldn't be Mr. Hardy. He's in the Bahamas." She hesitated, then said, "The Dolphin Bay Country Club. Room 417."

I shook my head. "There's no one by that name registered at the Dolphin Bay Country Club. There isn't even a room with that number."

She stared at me uncomprehending. "Are you certain?" She asked in a shaky voice.

"Yes." I paused a moment, then continued, "That was the number you gave me. There was no John Hardy registered."

"But . . . he called." Her black eyes stared at me in disbelief.

I shook my head. "He wasn't there."

Abruptly she reached for a pack of Virginia Slims on the coffee table. "I . . . ah . . . would you like some coffee?"

I could see my announcement had shaken her. Quickly, I rose. "Let me. In the kitchen?"

She fumbled to fish out a cigarette. "Yes."

I found the cups and filled them from a half-full carafe on the warmer. The coffee was pure Cajun—black, strong, and thick as cane syrup. Let it cool, and it would jell. "Anything in yours?"

"No . . . no. Thanks."

I sat the cup in front of her. She smiled nervously at me. "Sorry. I didn't mean to play the helpless female."

I smiled. "Forget it. It was a shock." For a moment,

I considered trying to reassure her, to remind her that there had been no positive identification, but I would be lying for I truly believed the body cut out of the alligator was John Hardy. The coroner's report would only reaffirm my conviction.

She picked up a book of matches and lit her cigarette. I couldn't help noticing she was a southpaw. She inhaled deeply and blew a stream of smoke toward the ceiling. She laid the matchbook on the coffee table. I glanced at it. Bagotville National Bank, identical to the book I found in the Suburban. And the matches had been plucked from the southpaw side of the book.

Laura Palmo laughed weakly and held up the cigarette. "Bad habit, I know. John and Marvin Gates have a steady battle going about smoking. We have a lounge at the bank. John doesn't smoke, but Gates puffs away like a swamp fire," she said, referring to the local practice of burning swamp prairies to refortify the soil with nitrogen.

I stiffened at her remark. Hardy didn't smoke! A thought leaped into my head. Well, maybe leaped is a little pretentious. Stumbled is what it really did, but still, if Hardy didn't smoke, then what was the matchbook doing in his Suburban?

My brain staggered forward another step. Could it have been the matchbook belonged to whoever killed him, if that had indeed been his body fished from Bayou Teche?

And if the matchbook did belong to the killer or the

accomplice, then chances are he, or she, was left-handed, like Laura Palmo. I shook my head at the ludicrous idea.

She released a long sigh, breaking into my thoughts. "Now, where were we?"

"Look, I know this is a shock for you, but if you think you can handle it, I do have a few questions I'd like to clear up."

She sighed wearily. "I'll do the best I can. It's just that I'm, well, the news has upset me."

"I understand. I'll be brief."

"Thank you." She smiled weakly.

"As I understand it, when he called was when he gave you the phone number in the Bahamas."

"Yes. Well, no. Not exactly. It was voicemail, but it was Mr. Hardy."

I frowned. "You didn't talk to him yourself."

"No. But it was him."

"You're positive?"

"Yes." Her bottom lip quivered. "It was his voice. I'd know it anywhere. He left that number where he could be reached."

"When you talked to him a couple days earlier—" I hesitated.

She supplied the date. "On the twenty-fifth. That's when he said he was going to the Bahamas. Two days later on the twenty-seventh was when he left the voicemail. It was waiting for me when I came back from lunch."

I sipped my coffee. "This is good. We don't have anything like it back in Austin."

Laura smiled faintly, but there was still a quiver in her lips.

"Now what can you tell me about John Hardy's ex-wife?"

She blinked once or twice, then drew a deep breath and closed her eyes. After a moment, she opened them and looked directly at me, struggling to regain her composure. "Janelle? They broke up years back. He never talked about her, but then about five or six months ago, she called him. I answered the phone. She wouldn't tell me what she wanted, but she was furious—screaming and cursing." She paused, and with a crooked grin, added, "She must be a Creole."

I thought of Sue Cullen and how enraged she had become—a typical Creole reaction. I chuckled. "You ever find out what it was about?"

She hesitated.

"Look, Laura. I'm just trying to get to the bottom of all this. We don't know anything for certain about Hardy. For all we know, he might have reconciled with her and told no one."

She snorted. "I don't think so. He made the remark that she could get all the lawyers she wanted, but she wasn't getting another cent from him. And then—" She hesitated. "Never mind."

I looked up from my notes. "No. Go ahead. What were you going to say?"

She grimaced. "Well, after Mr. Hardy made the re-mark about lawyers, he said she had threatened to kill him if he tried to beat her out of the money she had coming to her."

Jotting down my notes, I changed the subject. "I heard he had some gambling debts to a casino owner by the name of—"

"Jimmy Blue. He owns the Louisianne Casino just the other side of Maida a few miles from Morgan City," she put in. "Yes, Mr. Hardy has, or had, some gambling debts. I don't know any of the details, but from time to time, Mr. Blue called and from Mr. Hardy's reaction, the news wasn't too pleasant."

"A considerable amount?"

"He never said."

"Did they ever have any business deals together?"

She hesitated a moment, her black eyes shifting their gaze to the cigarette in her hand. "Not any with the Bagotville National Bank other than his casino is one of our depositors."

She seemed to be getting over her little attack of nerves. "Did you ever hear any talk about Hardy de-claring bankruptcy for another bank he owned years ago up in Opelousas?"

She shrugged. "Not really. Oh, there was talk, but I never heard any details."

"What about the name Babin? Hardy ever mention the name to you?"

For a fleeting second, she stiffened, then relaxed, so

quickly I chalked it up to my imagination. "A bank customer?"

"No. From what I heard, he was a partner of Hardy's fifteen or twenty years back. Committed suicide."

Her eyes glittered coldly. "I never heard of him, sorry."

"Babin had a wife, Karen."

Laura took a deep drag on her cigarette. "Sorry."

I remembered the call girl Sue Cullen had mentioned. "What about a woman named Fawn Williams?"

Giving her head a sharp shake, Laura Palmo smiled derisively. The coal-black hair that lay over her left cheek flipped back momentarily, revealing a large scar from the middle of her cheek to her ear. It was a burn scar. Once you've seen one, you never forget how the trauma contracts the flesh into leathery, irregular patterns. "Fawn Williams," she replied in disgust. "That's one name I've heard too much."

"Oh, why is that?"

She gestured with her Virginia Slim clutched between slender fingers that curved gracefully upward beyond the horizontal plane of her hand. With a sigh, she continued, "John, well, he, ah, he patronized her, I guess is the best way to put it. Often," she added with a wry grin.

"Over what period of time? I mean, a few weeks, months—"

She laughed. "How about years? Anyway, it came to a head a few months back when she tried to blackmail him. Threatened she'd go to the local newspaper with the story of their affair if he didn't pay off." She arched an eyebrow. "I suppose she's over the hill now and looking for security in her old age."

I arched an eyebrow. Sounded like motive to me. And the gas receipt in Williams' Jeep dated April 26th screamed opportunity. "What kind of payoff?"

"Five hundred thousand," she replied simply.

I whistled softly.

"But John refused. You see, Fawn didn't know just how connected John Hardy is, I mean—" She hesitated, frowned, then continued, "Is all up and down Bayou Teche, from Morgan City to Lafayette. All John had to do was call the Terrechoisie Parish Sheriff's Department, and they brought about some pressure on her." She shrugged. "I don't know what, but when they did, that little woman backed away in one big hurry."

"That was the last time she spoke to him?"

She gave her head a brief shake. "As far as I know. Oh, he did say that she called him back and swore to get even with him for turning the law on her."

Nodding slowly, I mentally went back over the questions I had planned to ask. More and more the answers and the facts, what few there were, seemed to be focusing on Fawn Williams, a.k.a., Sophie Mae Brown.

Laura drained the last of her coffee and stubbed out the Virginia Slim in the ashtray. She looked up at me questioningly, as if asking if the Q & A session was over.

I decided to see if I could sandwich Gates in before I visited Fawn Williams. "I've asked all I can think of. I know this has been a strain on you, but I do appreciate your time. One more favor. What are the chances of Mr. Gates seeing me on a Sunday?"

A faint sneer touched her lips. "Gates? Who knows, but let's find out."

Chapter Eleven

I went back over our conversation on the way to Gates' place. Palmo had filled in a few gaps, but I was still muddling about with no clear direction in mind.

Call it serendipity, call it chance, call it blind luck, but I've noticed that sometimes during investigations ideas or information surface unexpectedly from unanticipated sources. Sometimes I know what to do with it; other times, I have absolutely no idea, and that was the feeling I had now.

In visiting with Laura, every time Marvin Gates' name came up, I sensed an undercurrent of resentment on her part. And I noticed while she addressed Hardy as either John or Mr. Hardy, she simply used Gates' surname when referring to him. I had the distinct feeling there was something out of place between Marvin Gates and Laura Palmo.

Thinking back to the cassette tape given to me by Hardy's mother, I remember she alluded to the fact that while Hardy and Gates were not personal friends, they did make a winning partnership. A vague idea tumbled about in the back of my head, but every time I thought I had it, it slipped through my fingers.

Wearing a garish Hawaiian shirt, baggy khaki shorts, and flip-flop sandals, Gates met me at his front door, his craggy face filled with alarm. "Come in, come in." He stepped back and held the door open. He glanced past me at Jack in the Cadillac. "Your friend is more than welcome to come in, it's cool," he said.

"Thanks, but he has the air going."

The tone in Palmo's voice every time Gates' name arose intrigued me, so I decided to get a grasp on what sort of relationship the two shared. As I entered the foyer, I said nonchalantly, "By the way, I'd like to compliment you on your secretary, Laura Palmo. She's very knowledgeable, and she's been very helpful."

His eyes hardened. "John hired her, not me," he retorted sharply. The icy edges on his words were palpable, so palpable that I knew immediately the two never met after work for drinks.

"But she works for both of you."

He nodded sharply, and then led me down a hall. "Is it true? About John? They found his body?"

"Like I told Ms. Palmo, it's too soon to know, but if it is Mr. Hardy, we'll find out soon enough."

He invited me into a living area large enough to take in three of my apartments with room left over to park my Silverado pickup. Two walls sported extensive entertainment centers, each with its own arrangement of leather couches. In the middle of the room, surrounded by plush leather chairs, was a large round table with a mosaic top replicating the LSU tiger, in the middle of which sat a lazy susan cradling several crystal tumblers and carafes of various whiskeys. Two or three partially filled ashtrays and a few match–books were spaced about the table.

Gesturing to a chair, he reached for a bottle of bourbon and held it up to me.

I sat. "No, thanks. A.A.," I added so as not to offend him, a not unusual reaction of many people in that neck of the woods when their offer of drink is refused. This was a country where wine and whiskey and beer were as much part of the scheme of life as coffee, tea, and milk. In fact, I have family members who consider boiled seafood, fried seafood, baked seafood, and a six-pack of beer as the four food groups.

He poured a tumbler of bourbon and ran his thick fingers through his thinning white hair. "I don't wish harm to no one, but I hope it's someone else and not John."

I decided to see just how honest John Hardy was with his mother. "Were you and Hardy good friends?"

The portly man arched an eyebrow. "We are partners." He stressed the present tense *are*.

Absently, I picked up a book of matches and toyed with it. "And work well together, I was told. A partnership many admired." Before he could reply, I added, "On the other hand, I've been told that you and Hardy were not personal friends. Now, they might have been mistaken. I don't know. I'm just asking." I opened the match cover and noted that the matches had been torn from the right side.

I studied him as he took a hurried drink of bourbon. His reply was brusque. "We didn't run in the same social circles, if that's what you mean."

I didn't push that issue any further. I discovered what I wanted to know. Mrs. Hardy knew what she was talking about.

Nodding, I replied. "It is. How long have you two been partners?"

"Thirteen years," he replied, seeming to relax as he slid into a plush chair. Long ago I had come to the conclusion that bankers deliberately used thick, luxurious chairs to put clients off-guard so they could hit them with usurious interest charges.

"Nineteen ninety-three," he added, downing half of his bourbon. "Good years." He shook his head, then leaned back in his chair. "Now, what else?"

I touched on some of the same topics I had covered with Laura Palmo and discovered no major fallacies between the two. Gates elaborated on Hardy's gambling. "I know Jimmy Blue. His real name is Jimmy Opilitto. His place is as honest as any of them. John and I argued from time to time about his gambling. He lost big, and my fear was that word would spread about his gambling losses and in turn the bank would suffer."

"Did that happen?"

A sheepish grin played over his face. "Fortunately, no."

"I heard Hardy had some business dealings with Jimmy Blue."

Gates pursed his lips and shook his head slowly. "Other than the casino is one of our depositors, none that I know of."

"You knew John Hardy once had a bank go under up in Opelousas?"

His face grew grim. "Yes. It wasn't his fault. It was his partner, or I should say, his partner's wife."

I leaned forward. "The partner, that was Babin, Duclize Babin?"

"Why, yes," he exclaimed, surprised. "How did you know?" He paused, then chuckled. "You've talked to other people."

With a crooked grin, I replied, "A lot of them. So, what happened with the bank?"

"Well, I'm probably telling you what you already

know. John and Babin started one up in the early seventies. Babin committed suicide in about seventy-nine or eighty, and his wife—I think her name was Karen—well, she took over his share of the bank. Then she started embezzling. Went on for a couple years before John learned of it. By that time, she'd soaked the bank for almost two million."

I whistled. "Two million? She must have had herself one good time."

Gates frowned. "On the contrary. Her lifestyle didn't change. The D.A. figures she socked it away somewhere, foreign accounts or something like that. Naturally, she went to prison." He paused. "I don't remember exactly when she was released, but the irony was that she was killed in a car wreck just after she was released. I don't think she even had time to pick up her stash of money. As far as I know, it's never turned up. Probably rotting away in some foreign bank somewhere."

I chuckled with him. "Fate plays funny tricks at times. One more question. Did Mr. Hardy ever say anything about bank customers, investors threatening him after the bank folded?"

Leaning forward, Gates rested his elbows on the table. 'Like I said, it wasn't his fault. It was Babin's wife—or widow I should say."

"Still, I'm sure there were some irate, even outraged customers who wanted to blame someone. And he was the most visible."

Gates nodded slowly. "There was one that John told me about. Man by the name of Collins."

"He have a first name?"

"Not that I know of. John only mentioned him once, and then only by the last name, but he lived in Opelousas. Ms. Palmo might have heard John talk about him. He came after John with a gun, but the sheriff's department took care of the guy. I don't know what happened to him." He arched an eyebrow. "Surely, you don't think—I mean, after all these years—"

I shrugged. "After several years in this business, Mr. Gates, I can tell you there are people out there who can hold a grudge forever."

"But it's been at least twenty years."

I just shrugged. "That's all some people live for."

He curled one side of his lip. "That's pretty cynical, isn't it?"

Grinning, I rose and extended my hand. "My granddaddy called it being honest."

Back in the car, I called Laura Palmo who agreed to see me once again, but only if I promised to pick up a six-pack of Big Easy beer if our conversation was going to last more than ten minutes.

On the way over, one of Gates' remarks popped into my head. "Partners for thirteen years." Now, I was no lawyer, but I knew enough to understand that there were partnership agreements, and then there were partnership agreements.

I hadn't thought to ask just what sort of agreement Marvin Gates and John Hardy had. There are many prison cellblocks that have housed more than one partner who had removed the other out of greed.

"Well," Laura Palmo asked, standing in the doorway. "Did you bring it?"

I handed her the plastic sack with the six-pack of Big Easy. She smiled becomingly. "That means we'll go back out on the sun porch." She turned and headed down a hall. Over her shoulder, she said, "Did you find out anything helpful from Gates?"

"A couple items. Not much. He told me about a man up in Opelousas by the name of Collins. He said you might remember the guy's first name. Seems like the old boy threatened Hardy years back."

She sat on the chaise lounge and gestured to the couch. "He's probably talking about Edgar Collins." She hesitated a moment, then popped the tabs on two beers and handed me one. "Seems like I heard Gates and John talking about him now that I think about it."

I frowned. "That's odd."

A tiny frown knit her brows. "What do you mean?"

"Gates. He said he and Hardy had talked about Collins once, but he didn't remember Hardy using the man's first name."

An amused smile replaced the frown on her face. "That doesn't surprise me. Gates is as forgetful as the day is long."

Jotting the information on one of my ubiquitous 3"×5" cards, I replied, "Thanks. Saves me a little digging." I couldn't help wondering if Gates had truly forgotten or if it were a convenient lapse of memory. Still, what could he gain by lying about an incident that occurred before he met John Hardy?

I glanced up at her, and she was staring at me expectantly. "Anything else?" she asked.

"Yeah. Hardy and Gates were partners. What kind of partnership agreement was it? Any idea?"

She studied the can of beer in her hand several seconds. "I'm not sure, but it was something like . . ." She shook her head. "I can't remember exactly. They were general partners . . . and then something about tenancy."

I jumped on her observation. "Would it have been joint tenancy?"

Laura ran her slender fingers through her black hair, revealing a portion of the gruesome scar on her left cheek. "I think so. That sounds like it."

I jotted my notes on a card while trying to suppress my excitement. General Partnership with Joint Tenancy—the right of survivorship. In other words, when one dies, the entire interest goes to the other partner.

If I'd ever seen motive, this was it.

"So, what next?"

I wasn't really certain. "Maybe run down to Maida

and see Fawn Williams before heading back to the coroner's office up in Lafayette."

"About the autopsy?" Her face was grim.

"Yes, and then on up to Opelousas."

She glanced out the window at Jack in the Cadillac. "Your friend looks bored."

"That's his natural expression. Don't worry about him."

She hesitated a moment, parting her lips, then closing them.

"What?"

She shrugged, her black hair falling over her shoulders. "I was going to say if you and your friend are around next Thursday, you might want to go to the annual festival down at Maida."

"Festival?"

"Yes. The Loup Garou Festival, held at the end of the first week of May every year."

My eyes lit. "A regular, down-to-earth Louisiana carnival? With dancing and everything?"

"With dancing and everything."

I thought I heard her put a suggestive inflection on the word *everything*, but I quickly chalked it up to my imagination. "It's been years since I've been to one." I snapped my fingers. "You can count on it. If we're here, we'll show up."

She smiled warmly, her eyes fixed on mine. "Is that a promise?"

This time there was no mistake of the promise in her tone. "Only if you'll save me a dance," I replied, doing my best to imitate Cary Grant, but sounding more like Don Knotts.

Chapter Twelve

After dropping the kitten off to Sue Cullen in Maida, I headed for Fawn Williams' apartment. That's when I got the call from Sergeant Jimmy LeBlanc. He was already waiting for me at the coroner's lab in the Lafayette Parish Hospital. "I'm on my way," I exclaimed, signaling Jack to turn around and head north.

Leblanc continued. "It be no pretty sight, Boudreaux. The 'gator, he break up the bones something bad, he do. Suppose he gots to do that to swallow the man."

Jack frowned at me after I punched off, and I explained. "They're already at the lab. The autopsy will probably be over by the time we get there."

*   *   *

123

An hour later as we reached the outskirts of Lafayette, Jack grumbled. "You getting hungry, Tony? I'm starving."

I pointed to a fast-food joint with the ubiquitous name, Cajun Burgers. "There you are. They even serve alligator burgers."

"Not me," he muttered.

"And order some water for the kitten." I caught myself and grinned sheepishly. "Sorry. I forgot we dropped her off back in Maida."

He shook his head. "You and your pets. You might say you don't care for them, old buddy, but you can't fool me."

"Well, as long as I can keep them away from you, they'll survive," I replied, laughing.

"I was drunk then. I didn't know what I was doing," he protested.

"Maybe not, but you killed a bunch of exotic fish when you mistook the aquarium for the commode."

He muttered a curse under his breath, telling me where I could go.

While we were waiting in the drive-thru line, I asked Jack if he was getting tired of tagging after me. "The truth is, I don't know where all of this will lead. If this guy in the coroner's office is John Hardy, my job still isn't over. His mother hired us to find him, or find whoever killed him. And either way, in all probability, someone out there is going to continue trying to scare me off. If you want to get back to Austin, I can rent a car. No problem."

He studied me a few moments, a look of injured disbelief in his eyes. "You're asking me to decide between going back to the exotic metropolis of Austin and the wonderful company of your ex-wife or staying here with you and dodging snakes, alligators, loopy garous or whatever they are, and guys who might be trying to kill us? Pardon the vernacular, Tony, but that ain't no choice. I'm staying with you."

And so it was settled.

"If we haven't got this tied up by Thursday, we're going to a Cajun carnival down at Maida," I announced.

"Maida? That sounds like fun."

I grinned. "They call the carnival the Loup Garou Festival."

He looked around at me in disbelief. "The what?"

By the time we reached the hospital, Jack had scarfed down three Super Burgers and a large bag of french fries while I had managed to take care of a Junior Burger.

Jack pulled into the parking lot and stopped. I opened the door. "You staying here?"

To my surprise, he replied. "No. I don't care about sitting out here by myself. Think I'll tag along."

Inside we found our way through a warren of hallways to the basement. A uniformed security guard stopped us at the double doors leading back to the autopsy lab. I explained who we were and pointed through the windows in the doors to Sergeant LeBlanc and another officer standing before another door. "Ask the sergeant in there. He'll vouch for us."

The guard pushed through the doors, and the smell of pine-oil disinfectant engulfed us, stinging my nostrils. Moments later he returned and allowed us in.

Sergeant LeBlanc came to meet us, eyeing Jack suspiciously. I introduced him. LeBlanc grunted and took me aside. He spoke softly so only I could hear. "Didn't you tolds me when we talked before that Hardy's mother wants you to find him or them what kill him. That right?"

"Yeah," I replied in a low voice, puzzled as to what he was leading up to. "But I wouldn't do anything without your okay. I hope you believe that."

A satisfied grin curled his lips. "That is what I wants to hear 'cause between you and me, I think someone killed the man. It don't look like no accident to me. Me, I can't do anything until it all be official, but you, since you are already nosing around, then you might find something we can use. Understand?"

I studied him a moment. "Are you saying what I think you're saying?"

His lips parted over brilliantly white teeth in

a broad grin. He took my arm. "What you think? Now, let me introduce to the one what found the body."

He looked around. "Emile," he called out to the other officer. "This is Tony Boudreaux. He cousin to Leroi Thibodeaux up in Opelousas. You remember Leroi. We was all freshman at LSU together."

We shook hands as LeBlanc explained, "Emile Primeaux here is with the sheriff's department what got the body and the ring."

Emile Primeaux was a head taller than Jimmy LeBlanc, and I had to crane my neck to look up at LeBlanc. I shook hands with the tall man. I guessed Creole, for his complexion was light brown. "Pleased to me you, Sergeant," I said, noting the three stripes on his sleeve. "You have the ring?"

He nodded, but made no effort to retrieve it.

I told him what I knew of the ring. "From what I learned, the ring is silver gold and has a cluster of three diamonds in the center."

Primeaux slipped his hand in his pocket and pulled out a silver ring. He studied it a moment, nodded, then handed it to me. "Like this?"

I turned the ring over in my hand. "Sure looks like the one she described."

A frown knit his brow. He reached for the ring. "Who you talking about that described the ring?"

"Laura Palmo, John Hardy's private secretary at the bank."

He nodded and slipped the ring back in his pocket. "Me, I stop by and see her when I gets to Bagotville."

Dipping my head at the closed door at LeBlanc's back, I asked, "Have you identified him yet? Is it Hardy?"

Primeaux shook his head. "Gots to wait on the dental records from the dentist. No face left. Done be dissolved." He shivered. "Them 'gators, that acid in there stomachs could eat up a bowling ball."

"But what about the ring? Doesn't that pretty much nail down the identification?"

Primeaux and LeBlanc exchanged amused looks. Primeaux grunted. "How many J.H.'s you suppose there be?"

I understood his point, but I replied, "Hundreds, thousands, but how many of them were around Maida and owned a silver ring with three diamonds in a cluster?"

LeBlanc chuckled. "Don't suppose too many. Still, we gots to wait for the dental records to be official." He hooked his thumb over his shoulder. "You wants to see him?"

At that moment, the coroner came out—an older man with a belly sagging over his belt, flopping jowls, dark drooping bags under his eyes, and a lit cigarette hanging from his lips.

Jack, who had been listening in rapt attention to our conversation, spoke up, his voice choked with shock and disbelief. "Is he really dissolved?"

The coroner paused in the doorway, frowned at Jack, then winked at LeBlanc. "What do you think?" he asked, stepping aside and holding the door open.

Jack's eyes grew wide. He gagged, slapped his hands to his mouth, and made a mad dash for the men's room down the hall.

Chortling under his breath, the coroner strolled down the hall in the opposite direction, touching a match to the cigarette dangling from his lips.

I grimaced. I'd seen my share of dead bodies, mutilated, mangled, burned to a crisp, but never one so macabre as John Hardy, or what was left of John Hardy if that's who indeed it was. The alligator's digestive process was highly efficient for the flesh, especially on the upper torso, the shoulders, and the head had simply melted away like ice cream.

Emile Primeaux cleared his throat. "This one's wrists was rubbed raw, like he was tied up and tossed in the bayou. Of course, we ain't certain 'cause we didn't find no rope."

I looked up at the tall lawman in stunned disbelief. "You mean, he could have been alive when—" The horror flooding over me choked off my question before I could complete it.

Primeaux stared down at me impassively. "The coroner, he say that there be no signs of wounds except them done by the 'gator, so we know he wasn't shot or stuck with a knife, him. Probably an accident, the coroner say."

In other words, there was no definite proof Hardy was murdered. "You think it was just an accident?"

Primeaux and LeBlanc exchanged guarded glances. "That's what the coroner, he say."

LeBlanc handed me a stack of pictures. "Dese be took when the Terrechoisie Parish boys cut the body from the 'gator." He shook his head and whistled. "I hope I don't never run across no 'gator that big myself."

The alligator appeared to be at least sixteen feet long. I grimaced at the pictures taken from several different angles, but in each, the dead man's body had been doubled backward over itself before being swallowed, the back of the head pressed against the heel of his boots. I couldn't imagine the tremendous force exerted to bend the human body far enough backward to snap the spine.

I shivered and closed my throat in an effort to force the rising gorge back down. I dared not speak. I simply handed the pictures back to Sergeant LeBlanc and headed back to the Cadillac for a cold beer.

When I reached the corner of the hallway, I froze. Terrechoisie Parish!

"Something be wrong?" LeBlanc called out.

I turned back to face the two lawmen. "Sergeant Primeaux. Are you from the Terrechoisie Sheriff's Department?"

"Oui."

"Would you happen to know Fawn Williams?"

He grinned at LeBlanc. "Suppose just about every-body know that one."

Taking a couple steps back toward them, I asked, "She ever have any trouble with John Hardy?" I nod-ded to the autopsy room behind them.

His eyes narrowed. "Why you ask?"

With a shrug, I replied. "I heard that she'd at-tempted to blackmail Hardy for half a million, but the Terrechoisie Sheriff's Department put a stop to it."

Emile Primeaux studied me several moments. "Me, I don't remember nothing about that, but that don't mean Hardy, he don't talk to someone else."

"Can you find out for me?"

Jimmy and Emile exchanged looks. Jimmy nodded. Emile cleared his throat. "Maybe."

Chapter Thirteen

I remember clearly Josepphine Hardy's words. "My son is missing. I want him found. If he has been hurt or worse, then I will triple your fee to find those responsible."

There was no question in my mind that I will continue.

On the way back to Maida, I called Marty with the information I had. "I'm certain the body is John Hardy, so I'll pursue the case as a homicide."

"Fine with me, Tony. Just cover your keister with them Louisiana police. They got a reputation for tossing folks in the can just to hear them rattle around."

"Don't worry about me. I'll cross all my T's and dot all the I's."

"And make me proud!" His favorite expression, and one that invariably drove me up the wall.

Before I visited Fawn Williams, I had Jack pull into a convenience store where I made a photocopy of the receipt I had taken from her Jeep a few nights earlier. I folded back the original into my wallet.

I blinked twice when Fawn Williams opened the door of her apartment. Slender and curvaceous with rich auburn hair falling over her honey-colored shoulders and full lips matching the color of her shiny hair, she was, unlike Laura Palmo had surmised, anything but over the hill.

And, she, along with probably hundreds of others, fit the vague description given me by old Jean Baptiste at Venable's Convenience Store—red hair, dusky complexion, and shapely. In fact, the outline the old Cajun had sketched in the air with the shrimp deveiner failed to do her justice. He should have curved in and out just a little more.

Fawn lifted an eyebrow warily when I introduced myself. She shook her head and started to close the door, but when I blurted out that I knew she had attempted to blackmail John Hardy, she hesitated, then reluctantly invited me in. "Blackmail is a harsh word, Mr. Boudreaux." Her words were edged with ice.

"Just repeating what I was told, Miss Williams."

"Probably from Laura Palmo."

I grinned. "I did speak with her."

"I'll bet," she sneered.

In my job I've dealt with many ladies of the evening, both retired and currently employed, and one thing that I discovered quickly was that not a one of them wore a scarlet letter on her chest. In fact, most of them were charming, excellent conversationalists, and bubbling with charisma, qualities essential to maintaining a lucrative clientele.

Her apartment was tastefully decorated with early-American appointments, none of which appeared cheap. She indicated a tweed-covered couch with white ruffles about the base. With a weary sigh, she plopped down in an adjoining chair and remarked. "I figured John was finished with me. What does he want now?"

The question caught me by surprise. Either she was a clever, cool liar or she was as innocent as the Vestal Virgins. I had not decided just how much I should tell her, so I just played it by ear. "He's missing. That's why I'm here, Miss Williams."

She pursed her lips and arched an eyebrow. Her response was cutting. "You've come to the wrong person if you think I've seen him, Mr. Boudreaux. Last time I spoke with that slime, he backed out of a investment fund he had promised to set up for me."

"Investment fund?"

A wry grin curled her lips. "That's what we called it when the son . . . when he first brought it up. He wanted me out of the business, so he figured that half a million or so invested properly would provide me the opportunity to start over. Then, when I questioned him about it later," she added bitterly, "it became blackmail." Opening a cigarette case encrusted with diamonds, she slipped one between her fingers, and with her left hand flicked on a lighter. Another southpaw.

How many of them now, I asked myself. Three? Cullen, Palmo, and now Fawn Williams. All three smoked and all three were lefthanders. Any of the three could have left the matchbook in the suburban.

She took a deep drag and then looked up at me under long, dark, curving eyelashes that must have taken at least an hour every day to mascara and crimp. "He's a lying, no-good—" She paused, and a crooked smile played over her lips. With a shrug, she chuckled. "I apologize. I swore I wouldn't let myself get upset over the shaft he gave me. It's over and done with. I can't do anything about it now. And John Hardy certainly won't."

She was composed—calm, polished—too calm and polished. I wondered if it were simply an act, a deliberate façade. I decided to see if I could break down her composure. "You could be closer to the truth than you think, Miss Williams. Mr. Hardy might be dead."

With a harsh laugh, she replied, "That, I can live with, Mr. Boudreaux. What happened? I hope he suffered."

I expected a reaction, but not the one I received. Her bitter response surprised me. "We don't know for

sure," I lied. "All we know is he's missing, and yesterday morning his suburban was fished out of Whiskey
River."

She took a deep drag off her cigarette and squinted
through the smoke at me. In a hard, cold voice, she
said, "Excuse me for not crying. Now what does this
have to do with me? Why are you here?"

"Two or three reasons, Miss Williams. I've been
hired to find him, and I'm talking to anyone who
might have had some contact with him. Now, you say,
you weren't blackmailing him. I won't argue that because I don't know. I was told it was blackmail, and
when Hardy informed the Terrechoisie Parish Sheriff's Department, you backed away."

Her eyes glittered with hate, but she said nothing,
which suggested to me the information Laura Palmo
had provided was accurate. "And then I was told you
later called him and threatened his life."

Her nostrils flared. "That is a lie. I never threatened
his life, and if he said that, he's more of a liar than I
thought. Sure, I was angry and upset. He made me a
promise, then went back on it. I talked to a lawyer
who was willing to take my case, but a few days later,
he called back and said he was too busy." She snorted.
"Too busy! My eye he was too busy. John Hardy got to
him. That's what it was." She glared at me. "Truth is, I
could kill him, but he isn't worth what it would cost
me. Satisfied?"

"Not completely, Miss Williams. You see, a red

Jeep Cherokee was seen on the levee with Hardy's Chevrolet suburban on August twenty-sixth. That was last Monday, the day John Hardy disappeared."

Fawn shrugged. With lazy confidence, she replied. "So? There must be thousands of red Jeep Cherokees around."

"I suppose there are, but how many of them filled up with gas five miles from Whiskey River on that same day?"

The slender woman frowned at me, obviously confused.

I handed her the photocopy of the receipt. "And here is the receipt for the gas, plus you'll note the license plate number, Louisiana FKW-395, which strangely enough happens to be the plate registered to you, or rather to Sophie Mae Brown."

The lazy confidence she had exuded vanished. She stammered, "W-Where—I mean—" Her cigarette dangled from her fingers as she gaped at the receipt. "I didn't . . . I mean, this isn't mine. I've never stopped at this place, wherever it is."

Nodding to the copy in her hand, I asked, "How do you explain the license number? And the old man who wrote out the receipt said the woman had red hair."

Adamantly she denied filling the Jeep. "It wasn't me. I don't care what some yokel says."

"Then who?"

She puffed furiously on her cigarette. "I don't know, but it wasn't me. I can prove it."

Arching a skeptical eyebrow, I replied, "You might have to if the cops get hold of this."

A thoughtful expression erased the anxiety on her face. "How did you get it?"

"The truth?"

"Yes. Why not?" She glared at me, her eyes defying me to tell the truth.

"I stole it from your glove compartment."

She gaped at me for several moments, stammering for a response. Finally, she exclaimed. "That's illegal."

I grinned. "As can be."

A shrewd gleam filled her eyes. She leaned back on the couch and eyed me smugly. "I could call the cops. You broke into my car and stole personal items."

"I suppose so, but then I'd tell them that you had paid me to clean up your vehicle, and I found the receipts. Who's to say which one of us is lying? Besides, then they'd have the receipt, and you'll still have to explain it."

Her eyes flashed, then as quickly as the anger flared in them, it died out, replaced with genuine concern. "I'm telling you the truth. I didn't fill the Jeep over there, and I can't explain the receipt, but I can prove I wasn't the one who filled it because I was at a business convention in New Orleans from Sunday, April twenty-fifth through last Friday, the thirtieth."

"Convention?"

Fawn leaned back, resting her head on the back of the couch. She pursed her lips. "If you know my real name is Sophie Mae Brown, then you know my profession." When she saw confirmation of her statement in my eyes, she continued, "I worked the National Portable Builders Convention in New Orleans."

I lifted an eyebrow. "And you can prove you were there?"

A smile that bordered on a sneer played over her lips. "I keep records for the IRS, Mr. Boudreaux." When she saw the surprise on my face, the smile broadened. "Oh, yes, I'm an escort service. I report income and pay my estimated taxes every quarter. I've even been audited, and I came away with a clean bill of health," she added with a mischievous smile on her lips. "I'm a good little girl when it comes to the IRS."

Clearing my throat, I said, "What you're saying is that you have proof that on the day that receipt is dated, you were . . . ah . . . occupied in New Orleans?"

Her dark eyes narrowed, then widened in amusement. "With a client. Yes, I have proof." She rose abruptly. "Wait here."

To say I was surprised was an understatement. On the other hand, keeping records was good business, despite the type of business. It's just that I didn't expect it from someone in her profession. At that moment, my cell phone vibrated several times. I ignored it.

She glided across the room to her computer station, picked up a day planner, and came back to sit at my side, enveloping me with the sultry scent of what I figured was five-hundred-dollar-an-ounce perfume.

She thumbed through the planner to April 26th. "Read this," she said. "See for yourself."

According to the planner, her business day began at 10:00 A.M. at the Chateaubriand Hotel; then a second appointment at 4:00 P.M. at the Lafitte Arms; and her last appointment at 8:00 that evening was back at the Chateaubriand. "That one concluded at just after midnight," she commented. "We visited the Café du Monde for coffee and powdered beignets afterward."

I glanced at her skeptically, and she rewarded my cynicism with a smug but very becoming smile and added, "That was quite a profitable day for me."

Only the clients' first names were listed along with the hotels, all of the establishments in the middle of the French Quarter. She looked up at me defiantly. "Well?"

The tone of that single word was telling me to take a hike.

"Impressive," I replied, nodding in true appreciation at her thoroughness, but the skeptic in me knew the thoroughness could have been pre-planned. She could have forged the planner as an alibi. I didn't think so, but I'd run across too many devious minds that could have come up with such a ploy. I pointed to the 10:00 client, Fred. "I'd like to talk to him."

"Impossible."

"Why? You have something to hide?"

Momentarily flustered, she replied, "No, but— You've heard of client privilege, haven't you?"

I grinned at her audacity. "I've heard of doctor-patient privilege, and lawyer-client privilege, but I don't think I ever heard of client—" I shrugged, and feeling my ears burned, lamely said, "and well, you know-privilege."

She arched an eyebrow in pure innocence and in a voice coated with smug disdain, said, "Oh? Well, I make them feel good."

I laughed at that. I liked Fawn Williams, a.k.a., Sophie Mae Brown. I hoped she was telling the truth. If I learned she had murdered John Hardy, I'd be sorely disappointed. Of course, she had motive. The problem now was opportunity. "I won't argue that, but—tell you what. I believe you." That was a lie, but I didn't want to make her run if she were indeed guilty. I wanted her to think I believed every word she said, or wrote. "You put me in contact with Fred here to satisfy my own mind, and I won't speak a word of this to the cops."

Fawn stood abruptly, strode over to her desk, and picked up an envelope. She fished out some canceled tickets. "Look, I really don't want to bother any of my clients. Here are my airline tickets from Lafayette to Baton Rouge and on to New Orleans. Look at the dates. I left on Sunday, the twenty-fifth, and returned Friday, the thirtieth. That should prove what I'm saying."

I studied the tickets a moment, then handed them back to her. "Anyone could buy these tickets. That doesn't prove you took the flight."

Her eyes narrowed. "But, it's the truth. I parked my Cherokee at the airport all week."

"Look, Fawn. I believe you, but I'm telling you how the cops will look at it, what the District Attorney would say. Let me talk to Fred. If you were with Fred at the Chateaubriand Hotel on the twenty-sixth at ten that morning, then you couldn't have filled the Cherokee up an hour earlier at Venable's."

She studied me several seconds. Reluctantly, she pulled a scrap from her day planner, scribbled a name, and handed it to me.

I read it, Frederick J. Turner, Washington D.C. I looked around at her, puzzled. "This isn't the Freder—"

Wearing the same smug look the cat must have had when he swallowed the mouse, she finished the question for me, "—the Frederick J. Turner, senator from the pelican state of Louisiana." She nodded. "That's him, the one and the same."

Smiling at the bewildered look on my face, she added, "Freddy has connections with the big builders. Between you and me, he's the reason many of them stay in business, and they're the reason he continues to be re-elected." She paused. "So you can see that he might be kind of sensitive about talking to you."

I grinned wryly. "Not as sensitive as if the media got hold of it."

She studied me a moment, then laughed. "Let me call him."

Chapter Fourteen

It was growing late in the afternoon when I left Fawn's apartment, but not nearly as late as it would be when I met the good senator at the Achafalaya Regional Air Terminal east of Lafayette at ten that evening. I was to report to security, and they would take me to him.

I glanced at my watch and decided Jack and I'd have time to run over to Mowata and see Hardy's ex-wife, Janelle Bourgeois. Being a Sunday, chances were the café would be closed. If so we'd have to run her down at home.

As I descended the stairs from Fawn's apartment, I checked the caller I.D. on my cell phone. Jimmy LeBlanc. I punched in his number. Still no positive identification. Hardy's dentist could not be located, so a positive I.D. would probably have to wait until the next day. Before he hung up, LeBlanc said, "You remember what we done talked about, you nosing around?"

I stiffened, expecting him to say forget it. "Yeah. Why?"

"Well, me, I talk to Emile. He says you go ahead. Him, he like me. He thinks it be murder. Just give us all you find."

A sudden weight fell from my shoulders. "Don't worry, Jimmy. You'll have it."

Jack was popping his second Big Easy beer when I climbed in. To the west, the sun was dropping below the buildings, and a soft red glow was beginning to light the late afternoon sky.

"Head out the interstate," I told Jack. As we headed west on Interstate 10, I pulled out my laptop, hooked up my cell phone, and e-mailed Eddie Dyson, my savior on more occasions than I could remember.

At one time Austin's resident stool pigeon, Eddie Dyson had become a computer whiz and wildly successful entrepreneur.

I've always heard that all one must do to be successful is to find his niche in life. Well, instead of sleazy bars and greasy money, Eddie discovered his niche for snitching to be in credit cards and the bright glow of computers. Any information I couldn't find, he could. There were only two catches if you dealt

with Eddie. First, you never asked him how he did it, and second, he only accepted VISA credit cards for payment.

I never asked Eddie why he only accepted VISA. Seems like any credit card would be sufficient, but considering the value of his service, I never posed the question. As far as I was concerned, if he wanted to be paid in Japanese yen, I'd pack up a half dozen bushels and send them to him.

Failure was not a word in his vocabulary. His services did not come cheap, but he produced. Sometimes the end is indeed worth the means.

I was hoping it would be this time. I needed background information for a handful of individuals so I listed each person with whom I had spoken. I also added Edgar Collins and Jimmy "Blue" Opilitto.

As an afterthought, I asked for details on Antigua Exports as well as La Louisianne Imports in Bagotville. And since his bill would be astronomical, I added the banks of St. Kitts and Dominica along with account numbers and routing numbers.

From Lafayette, we headed west to Rayne where we turned north. Several miles up a narrow farm road lined by rice fields surrounded by levies, we reached Branch and turned west to Mowata.

Moise Deslatte hadn't been too far off when he told me there was only one of anything in Mowata. There was one general store, one church, one welding shop, one blinking signal light. There were two cafés, but then I saw one was boarded up. So, I guess he was right. One of everything. By now, the sun had set, and dusk was falling over the farming community.

To my surprise, lights were on in Lege's Café. "Pull in there," I said.

"Good. I'm hungry," Jack muttered, pulling into the empty lot in front of the café. A battered Chevrolet Caprice sat at the side of the small building. "How long do you figure on being here? I gotta eat something."

"Just so we're back at the airport by ten."

A thin woman with her hair pulled back severely and fastened with a rubber band peered through a serving window in the wall behind the counter. Steam rose around her. She smiled. "Find a table, you. I be right there."

A counter with a half dozen stools lined one wall. Five bare tables filled the remainder of the small café, all empty. We took the one closest to the kitchen. The rich smell of home cooking hung in the air, and Jack smacked his lips. "If their stuff tastes as good as it smells, you might never get me out of here."

The small woman came around the corner of the counter with two glasses of water in one hand and two menus in the other. She wore a red plaid short-sleeve shirt, baggy jeans, and sandals. Slapping the menus down and sliding the water in front of us without spilling a drop, she greeted us. "Hello, there, boys. You be new here in Mowata, huh?"

"Passing through," I replied, searching for a nametag, but seeing none. She appeared to be in her fifties, maybe early sixties, and typical of most farm women, she appeared to have been used pretty hard by life.

Jack sniffed the air. "What smells so good?"

Her eyes lit. "That be the speciality of the day, beef stew in thick gravy. We gots some left." She indicated the teakettle-shaped clock on the wall. "We be closing up soon."

"Bring me a bowl of that stew," Jack exclaimed. "A big bowl."

She frowned at him.

I laughed. "A plate will do."

A smile replaced the frown. "There you be. I comes right back with the stew. Fresh bread and home-churned butter. What you drink? Sweet tea?"

"Fine."

Jack frowned at me. "Plate? I wanted stew."

"Just wait. Cajun stew is a little different than what you're used to."

He leaned across the table and glanced at the door through which she had disappeared. "If that's her, it's sure hard to believe she was married to a banker."

I shrugged. "Never can tell. Get her in a beauty shop, some nice clothes, and you might be surprised."

Before he could reply, she returned with two large platters heaped with steaming rice and covered by succulent thick brown gravy that smothered chunks of tender beef, wedges of potatoes, and carrots, topped by fresh green hot peppers, and plopped them down in front of us. Jack's eyes grew wide. "All that?" he whispered.

"All that," I laughed.

When she returned with hot sauce, onions, hot bread, and sweet tea, I asked her if she was Janelle Bourgeois.

Her smile faded. "What for you wants to know?"

Her eyes grew cold when I told her John Hardy was missing. I continued, "I thought you, since you were once married, might have heard from him."

She snorted. "That one, he worthless. I worked my fingers to the bone helping him set up the bank in Opelousas. Den he gets too good for me and divorces me. Three years ago, he stopped my alimony." She grunted. "Wasn't much, only five hundred a month." She shook her head sharply. "He ain't no good."

I introduced myself and explained why I was here. "You have time to talk?" I glanced around the empty café.

Janelle Bourgeois studied me a moment, then shrugged. "Why not?" She gestured to the empty room. "We ain't exactly turning customers away." She laughed as she poured herself a cup of thick coffee and plopped down in a chair across the table and

promptly lit a cigarette. I breathed a sigh of relief. Finally, one who wasn't a southpaw. "Now, whats you want to know?"

"Last Sunday and Monday. Were you working?"

"Mais non," she replied immediately. "Me, I been visiting the old ones down in Maida. Lege, he own this place. Lege, he lets me take off three, four days. I come back last night." She studied me a moment. "You say this all abouts that no-good ex-husband of mine?"

I suppressed the excitement coursing through me when she replied she had been in Maida. "Yes."

She chuckled. "That one, he do alls he can to keep from paying me what he done owes me."

"Where did you stay in Maida, with your parents?"

"Mais non. The old ones, dey be in the old folks homes, you know, them places that takes care of the old ones."

"Nursing home?"

"Oui. Nursing home." She took a drag off her cigarette. "Me, I stays with my cousin, Louise Babeaux. She was Bourgeois until she marry Felix Babeaux, her." She shook her head and sighed. "I been gone from there long time. It be changing. The ones I used to know don't live there no more."

"Things do have a way of changing, Ms. Bourgeois, I—"

She interrupted. "Call me Nell. Dey all do."

"All right, Nell. I was told that you threatened to kill John Hardy if he didn't pay you what he owed."

The faint smile on her thin, wrinkled lips tightened into a scowl. She replied heatedly, "Me, I don't say that to the man. If he say that, he be liar. Who tell you I say that?"

I gave her an apologetic smile. "I can't say. I probably misunderstood," I added hastily, not wanting to antagonize her.

"I tells you what," she said, reaching into the pocket of her jeans and withdrawing a worn four-inch Case knife. "Me, I be mad enough to make that one a gelding. Mais non, there be no way I kill the man. For only eighteen thousand dollar, I not be going to no jail." She flipped open the blade to punctuate her remark.

Jack's fork paused between his open lips. His eyes bulged at the light reflecting off the wicked blade of Nell's knife.

"That's how much he owes you?"

Her eyes glittered with rage. She picked up a napkin and drew the blade down the middle of it, slicing it open without effort. "Oui. And to a po' Cajun like me, that a lot of money, but not enough to kill him for." She jabbed the blade in our direction for emphasis.

Jack jumped back. She laughed and closed the knife.

"By the way," I said, changing the subject, "you remember a boy you grew up with, Moise Deslatte?"

Her weathered face lit with memories of years past, and for a fleeting moment, I was staring at the soft round face of a young woman with stars in her eyes.

She closed the blade, and Jack went back to his meal. "Oui. That Moise. We be childhood *bien-aimés,* sweethearts." Her eyes took on a faraway look. After a few moments, she shook her head and came back to the present. "That long, long time ago, that was."

The scraping of a plate on the tabletop broke into our conversation as Jack shoved his empty plate away. "That was delicious," he announced, grinning nervously at Janelle Bourgeois. "Why don't you come to Austin and let me open up a café for you. We'll make a fortune."

The small woman beamed and, her cigarette clutched between two nicotine-stained fingers, waved at Jack, scoffing at him for teasing her. "Mais non. I goes with you, what dese around Mowata do?"

I had more questions I could have asked, but she had given me more than I expected. Besides, we just had time to get back to the airport and meet with the good senator.

She frowned at my stew. "You don't eat."

"How about a doggy bag," I said. "I'll eat back at the motel."

She nodded and headed for the kitchen.

Jack called out. "While you're back there, why don't whip me another dinner to go."

Nell Bourgeois laughed over her shoulder.

The night was warm, so Jack lowered the top on the Cadillac before we drove way.

Winding along the narrow asphalt roads back to the interstate a few minutes later, Jack remarked, "She doesn't look like she'd ever been married to a banker, you know?"

"I know. Maybe that's why Hardy dumped her."

"You think she killed him?"

Staring at the oncoming headlights, I replied, "They don't know if it's Hardy or not."

He snorted. "I'm no lawman, but you know as well as me that—" He shivered. "That body was John Hardy."

I chuckled and lay my head back on the seat, staring at the stars overhead. "Yeah. It's Hardy. The ring clinched it for me."

"Well, then, do you think she did it? They found the body in the bayou down by Maida. She was there. She admitted it. And you said she threatened to kill him if he didn't give her what he owed."

Turning my head on the seat to stare at Jack, I replied, "She might have been perfectly willing to use that knife of hers on him in the manner she suggested, but I don't think she killed him. She denied it, and in no uncertain terms."

Jack grunted. "Wouldn't anyone who was guilty?"

He had a point. "They'd have to be mighty clever to be as convincing as she was. Do you think she killed him?"

Pursing his lips, Jack considered my question. Finally, he shook his head. "No. She struck me as a

plain, down-to-earth farm woman who wouldn't lie to save her own soul."

Security at Atchafalaya Air Terminal sent us to the maintenance gate at the east end of runway ninety. "Park your car just outside the gate. The airplane will taxi to you." The craggy-faced security guard pointed through one of the expansive windows toward a line of red lights. "Down there."

Exactly two minutes before the hour we parked and turned off the headlights. The pulsating glow of lights lining the taxi strip illumined our faces with an on-again, off-again red blush. Precisely one minute later, running lights curved into the approach and landing lights flashed on. A minute later, an Astra SP with swept-back wings and the logo, National Builders Corporation, braked to a halt fifty yards from us.

The door just behind the cockpit swung up and stairs hissed down. A burly man in a suit stopped in the open door and waved for me to come in.

Five minutes later, I stood in front of the Cadillac watching the jet curve gracefully into the night sky and began a gradual turn that would take it back to the east. I could feel the heat radiating from the cooling engine of the big car.

"Well," Jack asked from where he sat on the back of

the driver's seat and peering over the top of the windshield. "What do you find out?"

Without taking my eyes off the jet now slowly vanishing into the night, I replied, "Somebody's lying, either Fawn Williams or Senator Frederick J. Turner."

"What did he say?"

Keeping my eyes on the Astra SP as its lights mingled with the stars, I replied, "He said he was on a fact-finding tour of the New Orleans' levees that day."

"He deny knowing her?"

"No. But he didn't see her that day."

For a moment, Jack remained silent. Then he whistled softly.

I nodded. "Exactly."

"She knew you were going to talk to him. She had to know you'd learn the truth. Why do you figure she went ahead and lied about it?"

The navigation lights of the Astra SP finally disappeared among the stars in the dark night. With a sigh, I replied, "No idea, but I plan to find out."

Chapter Fifteen

I climbed back in the car, and Jack slid down behind the wheel. "How tired are you, Jack?"

In the pulsating red glow of the taxi lights, I saw the weariness in his face, but all he said was, "Why?"

"How about a fast trip up to Opelousas? About thirty or forty miles from Lafayette. We can get a motel there for the night."

"Fine with me," he said, leaning over the back of the seat and pulling out a cold bottle of Big Easy beer. "You want one?"

I started to refuse, but I was exhausted. The day had been interminably long. It seemed like it was two months ago since we chased the cottonmouth from our room. "Why not? Maybe it'll wake me up."

I had Jack pull up at the guard's gate at the parking

lot before leaving. The uniformed guard came to the open door. "Yes, sir."

"By any chance were you working last week?"

He nodded.

"Did you happen to see a red Jeep Cherokee leave here last Sunday or Monday?"

His eyes narrowed. "You don't look like the law. Who you be?"

"No. Just a private investigator trying to find out something about the Jeep."

He shrugged. "I didn't work Sunday, but Monday a red Jeep Cherokee came in late and parked. The driver was a woman with red hair. She wents into the terminal. Real looker. I never saw her come out. The Jeep, it stayed there the rest of the week."

"Are you sure it was a Cherokee?"

He grinned. "Me, I been looking to buy one. One just like that one."

By eleven fifteen, we were ensconced in a clean, but plain room at the Jean LaFitte Motel on the second floor. This time I made sure the door was locked and the safety chain engaged securely.

For a moment, I considered calling my cousin, Leroi Thibodeaux. I hadn't seen him since just before Christmas at the funeral of his son, Stewart, who stayed with me in Austin until he found a job. Unfortunately that job was dealing drugs, and Stewart, the poor, dumb kid, ended up in the morgue.

"At least," said Danny O'Banion, an old friend in Austin and a concierge for the concierges of the mob, a sort of lower-level liaison between those at the top and the soldiers at the bottom, remarked, "at least you know where he's buried. No way you can put out flowers on Loop 360," he added, referring to the ongoing road construction around Austin rumored to provide free burial plots for those who ran afoul of the mob.

I didn't question him. Word had it that more than one missing person rested peacefully beneath the three feet of concrete that the great state of Texas called Loop 360.

The hour was late; I decided to wait until the next day to call Leroi. I really wanted to see that rascal. We grew up together, inseparable despite the difference in our races, but then, race was something we never thought of. We were simply cousins and good friends. His mama and my uncle, Patric Thibodeaux, had married against the wishes of both families.

Leroi and I had what I still consider an idyllic youth. We hunted and fished together, went to the movies together, and were constantly at each other's houses, although he did spend most of the time at mine since his mama, Lantana, had died in childbirth.

To my disgust that night I lay awake for an hour listening to Jack snore like a chainsaw with a bad spark plug while trying to figure out just where I stood in my investigation.

I knew the corpse in the coroner's office was Hardy. Obviously, so did Jimmy LeBlanc and Emile Primeaux. Otherwise why would they encourage me to investigate it as a murder?

If it were murder, then I had perhaps two, maybe three suspects, Nell Bourgeois, Fawn Williams, and Moise Deslatte.

Nell Bourgeois had motive, eighteen thousand dollars worth, and she was in Maida at her cousin's the day Hardy disappeared, April 26. She could have enlisted her cousin, Louise Babeaux to drive one of the vehicles to Whiskey River, and the two could have returned the Cherokee to the air terminal's parking lot. Both opportunity and motive. On the other hand, why use Fawn Williams' Cherokee? A random choice? That didn't make sense.

Still, as Nell Bourgeois had said, eighteen thousand is not enough to pay for twenty or thirty years in prison.

Fawn Williams claimed she had been jilted out of a half-million-dollar investment fund. That amount was more than enough motive. And she and her accomplice could have parked a vehicle in the vicinity of Venable's convenience store earlier. The two could have run the Suburban into the river, driven back to the convenience store where Williams filled up the Cherokee before heading for New Orleans in a rented car, while her co-conspirator could have driven the

Cherokee back to the airport. Again both motive and opportunity.

Moise Deslatte was hot-blooded, and to be shot at and accused of cheating was not the kind of insult a Cajun forgot. After talking to him, I didn't believe his motive was as compelling as the two women's, but still, the Cajun penchant for violence as a solution for many disagreements stems from before the dispersal of the Acadians from Nova Scotia and still runs in their blood. The years might have diluted the intensity of the emotion, but given the right set of circumstances, it could erupt in brutal anger.

Since Deslatte had spent the night in the bar of the hunting lodge, he could have sent his alligator-hunting goons, Juju and Marcel, to carry out the plot. The only problem was the same as Janelle Bourgeois. Why use Fawn Williams' Cherokee? Still, I had a good argument for motive and opportunity.

I finally dropped off to sleep, and in my dreams, a monstrous alligator was chasing me.

Next morning I tried calling Leroi, but there was no answer. Muttering a soft curse, I began searching for Edgar Collins in the Opelousas phone directory. There were thirty-seven Collins in the directory.

"There's as many Collins here as Boudreauxs," Jack remarked. "You sure Collins isn't a Cajun name?"

I rolled my eyes and started dialing the E. Collinses.

The fourth E. Collins knocked me back on my heels. "No, sir, it ain't me, but I gots me a older cousin who went by Edgar twenty or so years ago. Goes by E.K. now."

After a few more subtle questions, I learned he had lost his life savings when a bank folded and moved to Maida.

Maida!

Stifling my excitement, I stammered out my thanks and surprisingly enough had the forethought to ask for a phone number in Maida.

Jack saw the excitement on my face. "You find the guy?"

I hesitated. "I'm not sure. This guy lost all his money when a bank folded." I eyed the list of Collins in the directory. "He could be the one," I replied, dialing the next number. "But I want to be sure."

Jack shrugged and went back to watching the John Wayne movie on TV.

By noon, I was satisfied. I checked my notes. No Edgar's except for the one in Maida who now used the initials, E.K.

I tried to call Leroi again, and again no answer. I left a message, and then packed my gear.

Before we left, I made one more call, this one to Sergeant Jimmy LeBlanc. I closed my eyes and groaned when he said, "We gots no dental records, my friend. The office burned to the ground last night."

After muttering a few choice words, I asked, "Now what?"

"Last I hear, dey done started checking DNA."

DNA! I muttered a few more choice words. Not only would that send Josepphine Hardy into a tizzy, but it would also take weeks to get the results.

"So," he asked when I didn't reply. "You remember what we all talked about?"

A wry grin played over my lips, and I shook my head at Jack. "You're still okay with me investigating it as a murder?"

"Oui. Emile and me, we can't, not until we gots definite identification. Just you remember, keep us informed."

"You got it."

"Where you heading now?"

"Maida. Got a lead on a man who might be able to help."

Ten minutes later, we pulled away from the Jean LaFitte Motel, bound for Maida. Jack had raised the top on the Cadillac, and the cool air from the vents was a welcome relief from the blazing sun. I planned to call Marty later and bring him up to date.

I didn't have to call Marty. He called me before we reached the city limits of Opelousas. "Old lady Hardy just called. A technician from the police lab showed up at her house. He wanted to swab her mouth for a DNA sample. What's going on over there?"

"I'm ninety percent certain John Hardy is dead," I announced.

"What!" He shouted, and I could see him now. He had probably jumped to his feet, his eyes bulging, staring at the receiver. If he wasn't already perspiring, sweat would begin rolling down his flopping jowls and dripping on his wrinkled shirt.

"There's a body. They found a ring that could be his."

"But what happened? The old lady is driving me crazy."

I hesitated and lifted an eyebrow at Jack who glanced at me curiously. "It isn't pleasant."

"I don't care about that," he shot back. "Just tell me what happened."

Marty gagged when I related the gory details of the discovery of the body in the alligator's belly. I suppose I should be ashamed of myself, but I took a sort of perverted delight in embellishing the details of the grisly death because I knew back in Austin, Marty's stomach was churning uneasily. I went on to explain about the diamond ring with the initials, J.H., and the new boots the corpse was wearing. "Unfortunately," I added, imagining I could hear his stomach gurgling, "you couldn't recognize the face because the alligator's digestive juices ate it away." Then I added the *coup de grace,* which was a lie, but I couldn't resist, "All that was left was his teeth grinning up at you and his eyeballs rolling around where his cheeks had been."

That last remark was all it took. I heard Marty start

to heave and then the phone went dead. I clicked off the cell phone and leaned back against the seat, wearing a satisfied, though somewhat guilty, grin at my little fabrication.

Jack shot me a quick glance. "What did he have to say?"

Giving him a wry look, I replied, "Well, he didn't say it exactly, but what he meant was for me to keep digging. You and I both know, the dead guy's John Hardy. Like I told you before, his mother hired us to find him or those who killed him." I leaned back and stared at the light-colored convertible top. "So now, Mr. Edney, you and I are investigating a murder, and a murder, to steal from Agatha Christie," I added with exaggerated drama, "a murder most foul."

He shook his head wryly and grunted. "Still the English teacher, huh?"

I grinned at him. "You know how it is. You can take a teacher out of the English classroom, but you can't take English out of the teacher."

Chapter Sixteen

As we wound our way along the Bayou Teche Scenic Byway, a line of dark clouds loomed up over the south horizon.

"Looks like some weather," Jack muttered, flexing his fingers about the wheel. He looked around at me in consternation. "It isn't one of your hurricanes, is it?"

I laughed. "No. Just a spring storm. If it had been a hurricane, the story would have been all over the TV and radio."

We hit the storm around two that afternoon, a steady rain that the dry ground quickly soaked up. There's something about the Louisiana swamps during a rain that carries me back to the antebellum days, lazy summer days spent on the veranda sipping mint juleps, watching the silvery rain slice through air laden with the sweet, almost palpable fragrance of blooming jasmine.

Mid-afternoon we reached Bagotville and pulled up at the bank. The rain had slackened to a drizzle. I glanced at Jack. I was beginning to feel guilty about keeping him away from Austin for so long, but I figured he'd let me know when he'd had enough.

Inside, Laura Palmo greeted me with a worried frown wrinkling her forehead. Wearing a neat, dark brown suit and a white blouse with ruffles about her neck, she rose to meet me.

"Hello, Tony."

I nodded. "Laura. Can we talk?"

She gestured to a closed door. "In there. The lounge."

Once inside, she turned to me, a look of concern on her slender face. "What's going on, Tony? The Terrechoisie Parish Sheriff's Department came by my house yesterday and asked me to identify John's diamond ring." She bit at her bottom lip. "Did that have to do with the body you told me about—" She hesitated, unable to form the words.

"We don't know, Laura. They can't make a positive identification without DNA testing."

"DNA? That means . . . Mrs. Hardy . . ." She closed her eyes and sagged to the leather couch. She pressed her hands to her face. "I pray it isn't John."

"What about the diamond ring? Was it John's?"

She nodded.

"You're certain? No mistake."

"No mistake," she mumbled. "No mistake at all."

I drew a deep breath. "As much as I hate to say it, if the ring was his, then the body has to be John Hardy. Odds are a hundred thousand to one that—"

The door opened, and Marvin Gates jerked to a halt. "Mr. Boudreaux. I didn't mean to intrude. I was coming for my hat." He touched his finger to his jaw. "I've got to have a tooth filled." He shot Laura an angry glance as he closed the door behind him. "Have they identified the body yet?"

"Not yet. They're checking DNA."

He grimaced. "I heard the dentist's office burned. Shame—we'd know by now if it was John."

I stiffened momentarily, then tried to relax. I joked, "News travels fast. It only burned yesterday."

The portly man frowned, then smiled reassuringly. "Yes, I know," he replied glibly. "Someone mentioned it this morning. I forget who it was. One of our customers." He grinned. "You remember the old saying about the fastest way to spread news—telegraph, telephone, tell-a-woman? Well, around here, it's tell-a-Cajun."

We all laughed. I nodded. "I guess you know Laura identified John's diamond ring. The DNA is just a legal formality to nail it down."

He drew his stubby fingers across his forehead. "I can't believe it." He paused, then continued. "John and I weren't close friends, but he was the best businessman I ever worked with."

Gates seemed sincere, but I couldn't help wondering if he wasn't already counting the money coming his way as a result of his partner's death. I fixed my eyes on his. "As I understand it, you and Hardy organized the bank based upon a General Partnership with Joint Tenancy agreement."

He blinked in surprise, and his face darkened momentarily. Quickly, he recovered. "Why, yes. A standard practice in the business world, Mr. Boudreaux." He glanced sidelong at Laura.

"I know." I lied, not wanting to put him on the defensive. "Out of curiosity, what would have happened it Hardy had been married? His family would have been cut out of the business, right?"

He licked his lips, and he laughed half-heartedly. "If he'd been married, he wouldn't have agreed to a joint tenancy. Nor would I have permitted him to," he added.

"So I take it you aren't married."

He cut his eyes briefly at Laura, then shrugged. "No woman would have me."

With a touch of impatience edging her words, Laura spoke up. "How long does the DNA testing take, Tony?"

With a sigh, I replied, "Weeks."

"Oh," she replied simply, a strange smile on her face.

Gates nodded. "So it will be quite some time before

we know for certain if it is John Hardy?" I could have sworn I saw a satisfied grin on his face.

"Yes. But as soon as I hear anything, I'll let you know."

"I'd appreciate that." He touched his finger to his jaw. "Now, if you'll excuse me, I've got to get to the dentist myself."

When he closed the door behind him, I chuckled. "I don't envy him. I hate going to the dentist.'

Laura laughed and tapped a painted nail against her brilliant white teeth. "I'm lucky. Never had a filling."

I shook my head. "You are the lucky one."

"So," she asked, "I guess this means you'll be leaving us?"

I studied her a moment, for some reason surprised she should ask, yet not knowing why it surprised me. "Not yet," I replied.

She arched an eyebrow.

I grinned. "Didn't you promise me a dance at the Loup Garou Festival next Thursday? I sure wouldn't want to miss that."

Outside the drizzle continued to fall from the dark clouds scudding past. I jumped into the Cadillac.

"Now what? Find a motel?"

"Nope. Let's go to Maida. Pirate's Landing. I want to talk to Fawn Williams."

During the drive to Pirate's Landing, I jotted notes on my cards, and I couldn't help wondering about the identity of the customer who told Gates about the fire in Lafayette.

Fawn Williams answered on the first knock. When she opened the door and saw me, a look of disgust curled her lips. She rolled her eyes, keeping one hand on the door and the other on the jamb, telling me I wasn't the least bit welcome. "It's you, huh? Now what? I figured you'd be satisfied after talking to the senator."

Ignoring the venom in her words, I smiled at her, then hit her between the eyes with, "I would have been if you'd told me the truth."

Her eyes grew wide. "What?" She sputtered. "I told you the truth, you dumb—" She uttered a few expletives my grandfather would have knocked me on my backside if I'd said them in mixed company.

"Sorry, but that's not what the man said." I glanced up and down the covered esplanade. "Do we talk out here where the neighbors can hear, or are you going to invite me in?"

Her narrowed eyes spit fire. "Why should I? You're not the cops."

I shot back. "No, but I'm working for them, and if you don't believe me, give them a call and see for yourself." I paused. I softened my tone. "Look, Fawn. Maybe there's some kind of mistake. I don't know. All I know is that your story and the senator's story don't match. Now can I come in?"

Coldly, she studied me a few seconds longer, and then with a groan of resignation, dropped her hand from the jamb and stepped back, opening the door wider.

Plopping down on the tweed couch, she reached for a cigarette. Her hand trembled as she touched the lighter flame to it.

I sat across the coffee table from her. "According to the senator, he was on a fact-finding tour of the New Orleans' levees all day."

She caught her breath and broke into a spasm of coughs. When she recovered, she gasped. "That's a lie. I was there at ten o'clock. You saw my appointment book. He's lying."

"Why would he do that?" I asked innocently.

"I—I don't know," she stammered. "But he is." Her voice rose in pitch. "I'm telling you the truth. Freddy is lying. I was there."

Either Fawn Williams missed her calling as an actress or she was telling the truth. So I asked her, "Why would he lie?"

She shook her head numbly, her cigarette dangling from between her fingers, the ash growing longer and longer. "I don't know. I can't believe he said that. Not Freddy."

"He did, and that means you could have filled the Cherokee at Venable's at nine, had an accomplice drive it back to the Atchafalaya airport while you drove a rental car on to New Orleans. Then you flew back on Friday and picked up your Jeep."

She stared at me helplessly, the hard exterior she had maintained crumbling.

It wasn't the pleading look in her eyes, nor the weary sigh that escaped her lips, but for some reason, I believed her. Of course, none of what I had uncovered definitely linked her to Hardy's death. It was circumstantial—fairly solid—but still, circumstantial.

Tears glittered in her eyes. She blinked them away and stared up at me. In a plaintive tone, she said, "I don't know what's going on here, Mr. Boudreaux. I don't know who killed John Hardy. All I know is I haven't seen him in months. He had enemies. He had dealings with Jimmy Blue and the laundries and carwashes. I don't know any of the particulars, but if he is dead, I didn't do it."

"Carwashes?"

"Yes. Jimmy Blue has several carwashes and laundries all the way from Morgan City to Lafayette."

"What did Hardy have to do with them?"

"I don't know. But, a couple years back after one of our . . . our appointments, he told me the laundries and carwashes were making him rich. That's when he offered me the half-million-dollar investment fund."

Rich? From carwashes and laundries? Impossible. But then an idea popped into my head and a half dozen random pieces of information suddenly came together.

I rose to my feet. "It may surprise you, Fawn, but I believe you."

Her eyes grew wide. "You do? Honest?"

"Yes." I shrugged. "I don't know why, but I do."

I even had an idea why Senator Frederick J. Turner might have lied, to cover his own indiscretions by using the time-worn, but still effective political stratagem of "deny, deny, deny."

I took the stairs two at a time down to the ground floor and walked rapidly toward the street where Jack had parked. The drizzle had intensified. The heavy rain splattered on the concrete and splashed in the flowerbeds. I paused beneath the second floor esplanade before stepping onto the sidewalk, waiting for the rain to slacken.

Maybe it's true that God looks after fools and children. Maybe that's why I hesitated.

For in the next second, a large red clay pot slammed to the ground in front of me, shattering into a thousand pieces and sending dirt and multicolored flowers in all directions.

I gaped at the smashed pot, stunned.

Suddenly the honking of a car jerked me from my daze. I looked around and spotted Jack double-parked in the street. Hastily, I moved several feet to my right and then peered from under the esplanade. Everything looked clear. I pulled back, moved to my left, and ignoring the rain, leaped from under the esplanade. Bracing myself for an impact, I dashed across the sidewalk for the safety of the Cadillac.

Once inside, I looked up, but as I expected, there was no one to be seen. I decided not to mention it to Jack. He was spooked enough as it was. The truth was, by that time I was beginning to get a little spooked. How did the person who dropped the flowerpot know we were at Pirate's Landing?

"What was that commotion? Sounded like something hitting something," Jack asked.

"Nothing," I replied. "Let's go."

"Where to?"

"Find us a motel."

As we sped away, I hurriedly scribbled out my note cards, muttering aloud as I did. Suddenly the banks in St. Kitts and Dominica made sense. Could it be a money-laundering scheme? Casinos, carwashes, and laundries were perfect funnels for drug money to be deposited at the Bagotville National Bank where one of the partners, perhaps in this instance, John Hardy, was also aware of the scheme. Maybe he was forced into it as a result of his gambling debts.

Could that be what was behind all of this?

"You look excited, Tony. What's up? What did you find out from our girl in there?"

I looked around at Jack. "I don't have a good handle on it yet. Once we get to a motel, I'll have time to work through it. I'll tell you then."

Chapter Seventeen

With the rain, night came early—and with it a response from Eddie Dyson. I printed it out on my portable printer. Quickly I skimmed the partial report, learning nothing new about Hardy's ex-wife or Fawn Williams.

Jimmy 'Blue' Opilitto was connected with Joe Vasco out of New Orleans, which was no surprise. Every two-bit hood in Louisiana answered to Joe Vasco.

In 1990, Edgar Collins received a seven-year sentence for attempted murder and was paroled in '95, and since then had been a model citizen.

Moise Deslatte appeared to be just what he was, the owner of Deslatte Construction, a successful company saddled with a sizeable loan from the Bagotville National Bank.

I wanted to jump up and shout when I read the findings on the import / export businesses. "Antigua Exports is registered as a business on the island of Antigua, but no physical facility exists. Same with La Louisianne Imports in the city of Bagotville."

"Son-of-a-gun," I muttered, looking around at Jack who was engrossed in a reality show on TV.

"What?" he asked, frowning at me.

I continued reading. Eddie's next statement told me I was on the right track. "Son-of-a-gun," I exclaimed once again. "The State Bank of St. Kitts and the Dominica Republic Bank are off-shore banks and members of the Caribbean Financial Action Task Force catering to foreign accounts. Depositors must possess local citizenship, which can be purchased from the island administration."

And then the next line put it all in perspective for me, almost. "The transfers are deposited in a single account at the St. Kitts bank in the name of Antigua Exports. Transfers from Antigua Exports are made to Dominica and from there to Antigua. The Antigua accounts divide into accounts for John Hardy, Marvin Gates, and Antigua Exports." At this point I was ready to jump up and shout, but his last line tossed the proverbial monkey wrench into the works. "On April 26, the John Hardy accounts were transferred to a bank in Nauru to the account of Joan Rouly."

Joan Rouly? Who in the blazes was she? And how did she fit into this gumbo ya-ya mix?

I grabbed my notes. I fumbled through them but I found nothing on Joan Rouly.

Jack saw the frown on my face. "Did you find something?"

"I don't know," I muttered.

Jack grew impatient. "Well, are you going to keep me in suspense?"

I looked around at him. "Two things. First, it looks like our John Hardy and Marvin Gates are mixed up in a money-laundering scheme. I don't know who with, but I'd guess Jimmy "Blue" Opilitto, the hood that owns the Louisianne Casino."

He swung his legs off the bed and sat on the edge. "I thought Hardy was dead."

I shot him a disgusted look. "Okay, Hardy is a *was* but Gates is an *is*."

"Money laundering. You mean drug money? That sort of thing?"

I nodded emphatically. "Exactly. When I prowled through the suburban back at the salvage yard, I found invoices and copies of wire transfers in the glove compartment. I copied the routing numbers and account numbers from the transfers."

"So? What does that prove?"

Pausing to sort my thoughts, I explained. "First, these wire transfers are what they call EFT's, electronic fund transfers, to offshore banks in St. Kitts and Dominica. When I sent my source the routing numbers, he discovered that the transfers went to a bank in

St. Kitts into the account of Antigua Exports. From there they were transferred to a bank in Dominica into the accounts of John Hardy and Marvin Gates."

He shrugged. "So, what does that mean?"

I held up my hand. "Hold on. Let me get it straight in my head. "All right, one other aspect. There was also an invoice from La Louisanne Import/Export here in Bagotville billing the Antigua Import/Export on the Island of Antigua for eighty-six thousand dollars."

He shrugged. "What's the big deal? Just two companies doing business."

"Bogus companies. That's the difference."

"I don't understand."

"All right, here's how it works—just theory right now, but with a few more answers, it could be fact. First, Jimmy "Blue" Opilitto owns the casino outside of Maida as well as carwashes and laundries all up and down the Bayou Teche Scenic Byway. Let's assume they all make deposits in the Bagotville National Bank. Now, the legitimate deposits are inflated with drug money. Then funds are transferred from the local bank to banks in St. Kitts. From there the funds go to Dominica in the name on Antigua Exports, and then on to Antigua in the name of Antigua Exports. Follow me so far?"

He nodded. "Yeah. So far."

"The funds transferred to an Antigua Export company are used to pay La Louisanne Import/Export an invoice worth eighty-six thousand dollars."

Jack stared at me blankly.

"That's the process. Drug money is deposited in a bank, funds are transferred to accounts offshore, then another transfer is made to a dummy company, a shell company, which pays another shell company in the U.S. When the drug money returns, it is deposited in the bank here under the name of La Louisianne Import/Export. Now, the money is clean. It's been laundered."

A frown knit his forehead. "Where do Hardy and Gates come in? Didn't you say money went into their accounts too?"

"They're skimming."

He studied me a moment. "But don't the banks have to report suspicious deposits? It took almost an act of Congress when I deposited fifty thousand dollars in the bank."

"Yeah, but you did it in cash. These are all paper. From what I've heard, there are over half a million wire transfers, EFT's, a day. How do you scrutinize that many? And second, what if someone in the bank is part of the scheme? See what I mean?"

His eyes lit with understanding. "Yeah, yeah. You think Hardy was the one at the bank that let the wire transfers go out."

I nodded. "Hardy and Gates."

Jack arched an eyebrow. "And they were involved with this guy at the casino."

"Jimmy Blue."

"Yeah."

An unsettling thought struck me. What about Laura Palmo, Hardy's personal secretary? After all, she could have been the one to actually make the transfer upon instructions from Hardy. Was she aware of the details? Or was she simply following orders?

Jack broke into my thoughts. "You said two things. What's the other?"

Shaking my head, I replied, "This is really confusing. Funds from the John Hardy account in Dominica have been wired to a bank in Nauru to the account of Joan Rouly."

"Joan Rouly? Who is she?"

I couldn't resist grinning at the irony of my theory. "I never heard of her, but it looks to me that whoever she might be, she's skimming from Hardy, who is skimming from Jimmy Blue." I scratched my head and stared at the paper in my hand. "Maybe I should ask Laura Palmo. She knows everyone in town."

Outside a crack of lightning split the air. Seconds later, Jack's stomach growled. He grunted. "Well, I don't mean to change the subject, but I'm starving. You ready to go eat?"

I looked around at him. I'd forgotten all about dinner. "I'm not that hungry. Why don't you bring me something—a hamburger, Subway, whatever. I've got a little more work I want to do."

* * *

I must have been living right, for just as Jack closed the door behind him, my cell phone rang. It was Charley Benoit from the hunting lodge. "Boudreaux?"

"Yeah."

"This be Charley Benoit. You say if me, I find something, I should tell you."

My pulse sped up. "You bet, Mr. Benoit. What do you have?"

"Me, I gets my telephone bill. I see on it that Hardy fellow, he made a call to Bagotville at noon, den one to Maida at five o'clock that afternoon and den another one to Bagotville at three o'clock that morning. Me, I don't know if you wants them or not, so I call."

By now, my heart was pounding its way into the heart attack range. "You bet I want them." I scribbled the numbers and thanked him.

After he hung up, I called the first number, the call Hardy made at noon. I received the voice menu from the Bagotville bank. That must have been the call Hardy made to inform his secretary he and his client were taking a jaunt to the Bahamas. The second one, at five, there was no answer.

I dialed the 3 A.M. number.

Despite the pounding of the rain, I recognized the familiar voice that answered. Laura Palmo! I thought fast. I couldn't hang up. She probably had caller I.D. "Hey, it's me . . . Tony. Sorry to disturb you. I meant to punch in another number." It was a puny lie, but I hoped she took it.

"No problem." She laughed. "I'm flattered that you were thinking about me."

"I am. And about our dance Thursday night."

After we hung up, I remembered that when I had spoken with her the day before, she claimed Hardy had called her on the twenty-fifth and again on the twenty-seventh. She mentioned nothing about the 3 A.M. call on the twenty-sixth. I shook my head. How could anyone forget being awakened in the middle of the night . . . unless they wanted to forget?

At that moment, another epiphany hit me. That first day she told me Hardy had completely outfitted himself with hunting gear, including a pair of brand new waterproof boots. I shuffled through my note cards to be sure I was right. There it was. New boots.

Then later, Charley Benoit told me that Hardy had arrived without boots. He had to buy them at the lodge.

Someone was lying. And I could see no reason for Charley Benoit.

Immediately, I went back online and asked Eddie for a background check on Laura Palmo, born in Minneapolis, Minnesota, as well as requesting the listed owners of the La Louisianne Import/Export and the Antigua Import/Export businesses.

Then I looked up the telephone numbers for E.K. Collins and Felix Babeaux. I wanted to interview them as soon as possible. To my surprise, Babeaux's number was the one to which Hardy made a call at five on the afternoon of the twenty-fifth, and Babeaux was also an in-law to Janelle Bourgeois, Hardy's ex-wife.

Still, if Hardy did call Babeaux at five, then perhaps Janelle Bourgeois had nothing to do with Hardy's murder. After all, even though she was in Maida on the twenty-fifth, Laura Palmo spoke with him several hours later—an impossible feat if Hardy had ended up in the belly of that monster alligator earlier in the day.

E.K. Collins answered on the eighth ring in a halting, thin voice.

"Mr. Collins?"

"Yes."

I introduced myself. "I spoke to your cousin, Ernest, in Opelousas, and he—"

He cut me off. "I know. Ernest, he called me. What you want? You some kind of salesman?"

"No, sir. I'm a private investigator, and I'm looking into the disappearance of John Hardy."

He caught his breath. "You've come to the wrong man, Mr. Boudreaux. Me, I don't see John Hardy in over fifteen years since he done stole almost three hundred thousand dollars my wife and me, we spent years saving."

"Could I come out and visit with you and your wife for a few minutes? I'm up in Bagotville. I could be down to Maida in fifteen minutes."

"My wife's dead, Mr. Boudreaux. She die fourteen

years ago while I was in prison. Dey wouldn't even let me go to her funeral."

"I'm sorry, truly sorry."

"That don't make no difference. Me, I don't want to be reminded of John Hardy, Mr. Boudreaux. I don't care about seeing you neither."

"Then just answer one or two questions for me, Mr. Collins." Without giving him the chance to refuse, I continued, "And I promise not to bother you again."

There was a moment of silence. "What questions?"

I relaxed. "When did you start using the initials E.K. instead of your given name, Edgar?"

He seemed surprised at the question. Reluctantly, he replied, "After I gots out of prison in '95 and moved down here."

"One last question. Can you tell me where you were on Sunday, April 25? Not this last Sunday, but the previous Sunday."

He paused. His tone wary, he replied, "Me, I be visiting my family in Opelousas?"

I frowned. "You mean, Ernest?"

"Yes."

"That's odd. I wonder why he didn't mention that you had visited?"

The old man snorted. "Probably because you don't ask."

With a chuckle, I replied, "Probably so, Mr. Collins. Probably so." I thanked him, adding that if necessary, I might have to call him once again.

After hanging up, I jotted my notes on a 3"×5" card, then dialed Felix Babeaux. I studied the card while the phone rang. With a wry grunt, I knew that even if E.K. Collins had not visited his cousin in Opelousas, there was no way I could prove otherwise.

Still no answer at the home of Felix Babeaux.

After I hung up, I pulled out all my note cards and laid them out on the table. I had over eighty, and I started reading back over them, one by one.

More than once in rereading my notes, a new idea, a new angle would hit me, sometimes a profitable one, sometimes not. This time I got lucky.

E.K. Collins had stopped using his given name, Edgar, after he was released from prison. I read the card again. Sunday, the day before at her house, Laura told me his name was Edgar. How could she have known if she'd only been with the bank nine years? Even if there had been any communication with Collins, he would have been using the initials E.K.

And then I remembered she told me she had over-head Hardy and Gates talking about him, but Gates claimed Hardy never mentioned Collins' given name, which could have been a deliberate memory loss on his part, though I had no idea why.

I leaned back and stared unseeing at the TV. I had put together three maybe four shaky, little theories.

Fawn Williams motive was the investment fund. And she had opportunity.

Janelle Bourgeois motive was the $18,000 back alimony. I still had to find out if she had opportunity, so I planned to visit her cousin next morning, specifically to see if she could not account for her time after 3 A.M.

Then there was Gates. He had motive with the money-laundering scheme. And he knew about the dentist office burning only hours after it happened. He could have ordered the burning. Opportunity? He could have hired someone.

And then back to the money-laundering scheme, which I hoped had nothing to do with Hardy's death. I wasn't crazy about upsetting any mob connections from Jimmy Blue up to Joe Vasco in New Orleans. Messing with mob money led to only one outcome, and it wasn't one I particularly relished. If it were money-laundering, I planned to turn it over to Emile Primeaux and Jimmy LeBlanc, and beat a hasty retreat back to Austin, Texas.

There was still Moise Deslatte and his two brain-dead sidekicks, Juju and Marcel.

My stomach growled. I pushed back from the table and opened the ice chest. I picked up a can of Big Easy beer, then hesitated. With a shrug, I replaced it and headed out the door. A Coke or Dr. Pepper would do just fine.

The steady rain continued, pounding against the roof. Out on the second floor esplanade, I placed my hands on the rail and leaned forward, studying the lights of the city and the reflection of headlights off the wet roads. For some reason, I thought of the loup garou. A perfect night for one. I shivered.

I headed down the esplanade to the soft drink machine on the landing at the head of the stairs leading to the ground floor.

As I turned the corner, I glimpsed movement in front of me and ducked. I felt a hard object graze the top of my head and heard it slam into the stucco wall of the motel with a crack.

I threw my arms up and out, knocking away the hand holding the club. In the same movement, I straightened my bent knees, springing upward and throwing a straight right.

My knuckles hit bone, and a muffled cry echoed in the stairwell.

Chapter Eighteen

My attacker tumbled head over heels down the stairs, and I lunged down right after him. He must've been part cat for as soon as he hit the ground, he bounded to his feet. Before he could take a step, I leaped on him, sending him sprawling to the ground with me on top and bouncing the back of his head off the concrete.

He grunted and went limp.

When I climbed to my feet, I froze. He was one of the two swamp rats I'd spotted back at the fish camp, driving the powerboat that tried to cut us in two. I looked around, but no one was to be seen. I dragged him back under the stairwell and leaned him up against the wall. "All right, wake up," I growled, shaking him roughly. "Who are you? Who sent you?"

He groaned. "No one," he muttered.

My blood boiled. I usually shy away from violence, but this cracker had been doing his level best to drive us away, or perhaps even kill us. Viciously, I slammed him face first on the concrete and jabbed my knee in his back while lacing my fingers under his chin and pulling back, curving his spine into a position it wasn't designed to take.

He grunted.

"Tell me," I hissed between clenched teeth. "Who sent you?"

Groaning in pain, he muttered. "Don't know. I—"

I yanked harder. "Don't lie. Who? I'll pull your head back to your heels if I have to."

"Awright, awright. You be breaking it. Pellerin! That guy's name, it be Pellerin," he groaned. "He the one."

I tugged hard. "First name."

"Don't know. Just Pellerin."

Pellerin? Puzzled, I relaxed my grip slightly, but it was enough for him to spin over, throwing me off balance. Before I could catch myself, he lashed out with his foot and kicked me in the chest, sending me tumbling over backward. By the time I leaped to my feet, he was racing across the parking lot into the darkness. I took after him, not ten feet behind.

He shot between two cars, then cut to the right. When I tried to make the cut, my leather-soled shoes slipped on the wet tarmac, and I went skidding on my posterior. By the time I climbed back to my feet, he had disappeared.

I stood staring after him. "Pellerin," I muttered, remembering Juju's assertion that when Babin's wife, Karen, was killed, her brother, Thertule Pellerin, disappeared into the swamps, supposedly bewitched into a loup garou by the local cauchemar. I shook my head wryly. Maybe the loony ran off into the swamps, but he had certainly not morphed into a loup garou.

Jack was in when I returned. He stared at my disheveled appearance in surprise. "What the—"

"A visitor," I said, stripping off my wet shirt. I related briefly the details while I slipped on a fresh T-shirt.

"What was he, a mugger?"

"Anything but. One of our friends from the bait camp and the boat that tried to cut us in two."

His eyes grew wide.

I nodded, figuring he'd be better off back in Austin, for it could be that things might become intense around here. "Look, Jack, I think you ought to go home. It's getting serious around here. I don't think they're kidding anymore."

He blanched, gulped, then set his jaw. "I'm staying, Tony. No way I'm going off and leaving you."

I could have hugged him at that moment, but I didn't want to give him the wrong impression. "All right," I replied brusquely. "Don't say I didn't warn you."

*   *   *

After Jack dropped off to sleep, I stared blankly at the TV, trying to figure out how Thertule Pellerin fit into John Hardy's death. His sister, Karen Pellerin Babin was dead, killed in a car crash just after she gained her release from prison. The only idea I could come up with was that maybe Gates had learned the brother's identity and somehow contacted him.

I managed to put together a theoretical account of what had been taking place. Gates and Hardy were stealing from the mob. The hidden accounts testified to that. Gates, becoming too greedy, had Hardy killed, thereby taking over his share of the bank in addition to his accounts. But someone else was in the mix, Joan Rouly, who was siphoning off Hardy's funds from the Dominica Bank to an account at the bank in Nauru, a small island three thousand miles northeast of Australia.

As much as I hated to admit it, the only logical bank employee with access to Hardy and Gate's personal information was Laura Palmo. I cringed at the idea, but there it was.

I pondered over just how I could get Gates to come clean. In a brilliant flash of inspiration, I knew. I'd simply threaten to tell Jimmy Blue.

Shaking my head, I turned off the TV and pulled the covers up about my neck. "You're reaching, Tony. Reaching too far. Keep it up and you're going to fall flat on your face."

During the early morning hours, Jack woke me up.

"I can't sleep, Tony. I keep thinking about how these people always know where we are. You keeping saying there isn't nothing supernatural about it, but I'm saying something is there. Something unnatural is doing all this. There's got to be."

I lay staring into the dark above my head. I had no explanation. I blew softly through my lips. "If there is, I don't know what it is."

After breakfast next morning, I called Gates at home. He was at a meeting in Lafayette and would return the next day.

I sat staring at the receiver, considering my next step. I had no luck contacting Louise Babeaux, so I decided to drive on down and get directions from a local. All I needed to know was if Janelle Bourgeois had disappeared anytime after 3 A.M. on the twenty-sixth.

But before I visited Babeaux, I wanted to stop in at the bank and talk once again with Laura Palmo. I was still puzzled over the early morning call on the twenty-sixth, the one she had neglected to tell me about, and I also had two or three other questions for her.

I felt a tinge of guilt in thinking she was involved, but over the years in my business, you become jaded and suspicious of everyone. Still I hoped she could shed some light on my concerns.

"You want to go with me?" I asked Jack.

He looked around from the movie on TV. "Where?"

"The bank, then on down to Maida."

"Naw. I don't care about sitting outside the bank, but I'll ride down to Maida with you. You take the Caddie to the bank and then come back and pick me up. Okay?"

Laura Palmo greeted me with a bright smile and a teasing arch on an eyebrow. "Still waiting for the DNA results, I see."

I grinned. "That's what they pay me for." I winked at her. "To be honest, I hope it takes the rest of the week. I've been looking forward to the Loup Garou Festival."

She smiled wickedly. "So have I." She rose and headed for the lounge. "How about some coffee? We can talk without anyone disturbing us."

I followed her eagerly, reminding myself she was probably not craving being alone with me as much as she craved a cigarette.

She poured two cups of coffee and slipped in at one of the formica-topped tables, and as I expected, lit up. "You get in touch with your party last night?" she asked, referring to the call I made to her.

"No problem."

"So, what brings you here?"

Her perfume drifted across the table to me. I don't know what kind it was, but the fragrance was pure Laura Palmo. "Would you be disappointed if I said I just came to see you," I replied in what I hoped was a suave manner.

She laughed, a bright tinkle. "Would you be hurt if I said I thought you're fibbing?"

I laughed with her. "No. Truth is, I wanted to visit with Gates, but according to his housekeeper, he won't be back until tomorrow."

A tiny frown knit her forehead. "I can put you in touch with him if it's urgent."

"No. It can wait until tomorrow, but I do have a couple points you can clear up for me."

Her features tightened almost imperceptibly. "Oh? Such as?"

"First, do you know a woman around here by the name of Joan Rouly?"

She pursed her lips and after a moment shook her head. "I don't know of any Roulys around. Not here in Bagotville." Her brow knit in concentration. "And I don't remember any down in Maida either."

I sipped my coffee. It was delicious. Thick, black, and syrupy. If I'd had a slab of hot homemade bread, I would have been in heaven. "I've missed coffee like this back in Texas," I said, smacking my lips.

"We have plenty of it." She indicated the almost full carafe. "Anything else?"

"Yeah. When we first talked, you said Hardy bought a complete outfit of hunting clothes, including water-proof boots."

Her eyes narrowed faintly. "That's what he told me," she replied. "I didn't see them."

That made sense to me. "And you said he called you on the twenty-fifth and twenty-seventh. Is that right?" I deliberately left out the call on the twenty-sixth.

She inhaled deeply and blew a stream toward the textured ceiling. "Yes, but you didn't mention the one on the twenty-sixth. He woke me up around three or so."

I played dumb. "The twenty-sixth? I don't remember that one."

"Oh?" She arched an eyebrow. "I'm sure I told you about it. If I didn't, I apologize. I hope I didn't cause you any problems."

"What did he want?"

She hesitated and glanced around. "I shouldn't say anything." Her cheeks colored. "I mean, if the ah . . . the man in Lafayette is really John, I'd feel guilty talking about a dead man."

I understood how she felt. "Don't worry about his character. If the call was important, I need to know."

With a toss of her head, she replied, "It wasn't important. He was drunk, and he was angry at one of the bank's customers. I tried to calm him down."

Suddenly two pieces clicked together. "You wouldn't be talking about Moise Deslatte, would you?"

She nodded. "Mr. Deslatte is a good customer. I'd hate to lose his business. He's one of the backbones of Maida, and he has a lot of friends up here in Bagotville."

That made sense to me, so I asked my last question. "Did either of the partners have offshore bank accounts?"

She frowned at me, a puzzled expression on her face. "You mean personal accounts?"

"Yes," I replied, watching her facial expression for any hint of deception.

She slowly shook her head. "Not that I know of."

I cringed inwardly. *Had she lied to me?* Just as I started to ask about the mail I had seen on her desk that first day from Antigua, she continued. "But, we do have a bank customer from Antigua, the Antigua Import/Export Company."

I sighed with relief.

She arched an eyebrow. "Anything else?"

"That's it," I replied. "Thanks for the coffee."

I drove back to the motel, relieved that Laura Palmo was not involved in the scheme.

Chapter Nineteen

The day was blistering hot, so Jack left the top up and turned on the air.

Just outside of Maida, we stopped at Zolte's Fast Stop convenience store to gas up. Jack pulled up at the pump and eyed the building warily. Zolte must have built it from hurricane debris, for almost every imaginable type of construction material was evident.

After filling the tank, Jack went in to pay, and I followed him inside for directions.

Three dark-complexioned men looked up from a card game. A small, balding man, whose wrinkled face looked like a plowed field, sighed, rose to his feet and shuffled over to an ancient cash register behind the counter.

"Good morning," Jack said cheerfully, handing him a credit card.

He shook his head. "Me, I don't take no credit cards. All be in cash."

Jack shrugged and pulled out his wallet.

The other two had been watching us warily. I had the eerie feeling that we had somehow stepped seventy-years into the past when cagey moonshiners eyed federal revenuers suspiciously.

While the old man made change, he mumbled, "You ain't from around hereabouts."

I spoke up. "Nope. We're trying to find out where the Babeauxs live."

Suddenly the two behind us started muttering to each other.

I glanced around, and they were both staring at us with wide eyes.

"Something wrong?" I took a step toward them, and both made the sign of a cross. I stopped and looked around at the old man.

He shook his head. "Babeauxs, that be bad place to go."

Frowning, I asked, "Why?"

"Babeaux's woman, she be a cauchemar."

I laughed, but the expression on the old Cajun's face told me he was deadly serious.

Jack almost gagged. "Tony, isn't that . . . isn't that one of those things you told me about? Huh?"

Ignoring Jack, I shrugged. "Can you give me directions to her place?"

He shook his head sadly. "Sometimes, men go out there, and dey not come back."

I arched an eyebrow skeptically. "We'll take the chance, but I would certainly appreciate it if you'd tell me how to reach their place."

Jack shot me a horrified look. "We?"

I ignored him.

Gesturing with both hands, Zolte gave me a set of complicated directions. When he finished, he wagged a bony finger. "Don't you be getting off the road for nothing. The loup garou, he can change from a tree and grab you. He bites you on the neck, and you be dancing through the swamps with the other werewolves."

Jack gagged. "Tony!"

I continued to ignore him. "Tell me, would you happen to know Louise Babeaux's cousin, Janelle Bourgeois. She used to live here."

One of the men at the card table nodded. He shoved his gimme cap to the back of his head. "Oui. Me, I know her from the time we learned catechisms."

The other one agreed. "Her, she come in here not long ago."

Jack grabbed my arm, but I brushed his hand away.

"Yeah," the old man behind the counter put in. "Her, she be driving old Felix's pickup."

Gimme Cap laughed. "Me, I don't know how that Felix, he keep that piece of junk running."

"About what time was that?"

The owner arched an eyebrow. "It be six that afternoon." He shook his head. "The day, I don't remember, but she was heading back into the swamp to her cousin's."

Jack whispered harshly, "I'm not going out there."

Continuing to ignore him, I asked. "Anyone around by the name of Rouly?"

They shrugged.

Remembering the name of the man who had turned the mugger loose on me last night, I asked. "What about Pellerin?"

The three Cajuns froze. One made the sign of a cross. "That be Thertule. He be loup garou. Babeaux, she done make him loup garou."

Jack started choking.

I forced a smile. "Thanks. Come on, Jack, let's go."

Outside, Jack started babbling. "I'm not going out there. That's what's been after us, a loup garou. That witch, she made him one. Didn't you hear those old men? That's how he always knows where we are. She probably told him."

I just laughed as I climbed into the car. "There's no such thing, Jack. I told you, superstitions, myths. Nothing more. Now, let's go."

He shook his head. "I'll stay here. You pick me up on the way back, okay?"

"Don't be ridiculous." I snorted. "Get in and let's go."

"I'm staying."

Shaking my head, I glanced at the swamps surrounding Zolte's. "All right, but remember what the old man said. Don't go wandering around. Stay away from the trees. Can't tell when one of them will turn into a loup garou and bite you on the neck."

A worried frown wrinkled his forehead, and he glanced over his shoulder. He grimaced. "All right, but I don't like it." He slid behind the wheel.

Turning at the first intersection in town, we headed for Bayou Teche. A few miles down the narrow highway, we spotted the Babeaux mailbox, which was twisted into a grotesque shape by high school kids constantly swinging at it with ball bats when they passed. We turned down a dirt road that wound through the swamp. The spidery leaves dangling high overhead from the ancient cypress cast a chilling gloom over the road that led ever deeper into the dark swamp.

A guttural *ga-rump ga-rump* sounded from the black waters off to our left, followed by several responses all around us. Jack looked around me sharply. "What was that?"

I couldn't resist grinning. "Alligators."

He gulped so hard that even beneath the fleshy folds on his neck, I could see his Adam's apple bobbing up and down like a perch cork.

Just then an egret shrieked, and Jack jumped.

"They won't bother you," I said, laughing. "Just don't go wading out there."

In a quaking voice, he replied, "You don't have to worry any about that."

"That must be it," I said, pointing ahead to a shack on piers over the waters of Bayou Teche. A wooden walk led from the shore to the square hovel surrounded on all four sides by a walkway. An old pickup held together by rust was parked on the shore. That must have been the one they talked about back at the store.

We pulled up beside the ancient pickup, an old Ford like my grandpere Moise drove back in the seventies. As we came to a halt, a small man squatting by the edge of the platform was pulling up a crab trap full of big blue crabs, their pincers clacking ominously. He looked around, then spoke over his shoulder to someone in the shack.

Moments later a tall, rawboned woman the color of swamp water stepped out onto the walkway. She wore a yellow blouse, a billowing, multicolored skirt that dragged the ground, a bright red do-rag about her short hair, and a scowl on her frowning face. Smoke drifted up from the corncob pipe between her lips.

She spoke to the small man who darted inside the shack and returned with a lever action rifle.

Jack wheezed. "Don't worry about anything, huh?"

It was my turn to gulp. "All right, stay calm. I'll get out and talk to them." As an afterthought, I added, "But keep this thing in reverse and the motor running."

He didn't answer, but I knew he was ready to stomp

down on the accelerator. I stepped out with my hands high and a big smile on my face. "Good morning," I called out, not moving from behind the open door.

The woman lumbered forward, her eyes narrowed. "What you want? We don't like company."

"I'm looking for the cousin of Janelle Bourgeois. Louise Babeaux."

The small man stepped up to her side, the muzzle of the rifle pointing in the general direction of my feet. Taking a puff off the pipe, she said, "Why you want her?"

I explained quickly. "Janelle Bourgeois said she visited Louise and Felix Babeaux a couple weekends back."

"So?"

"Are you Mrs. Babeaux?"

"Might be."

"Well, ma'am, all I want to do is to verify that she was here."

She frowned. "Ver . . . what?"

"I just want to make sure she was here."

"Why you want to know?"

I lied. "There was a man murdered up in Mowata. She said she was here when it happened."

"Oui. Nell, she be here."

Suppressing a grin, I asked, "On the twenty-fifth and twenty-sixth?"

"Oui."

I told another little lie. "She said she borrowed your pickup. Can you tell me how long she was gone?"

The two of them just stared at me. Finally, after what seemed like an hour, Louise replied, "Maybe two hour."

The small man chimed in. "That woman, she broke up that old truck. That thing, it ain't run since." He nodded to his wife. "Us, we work on it all the night."

"Janelle too?"

He nodded emphatically. "She be the one that broke it. She gots to help."

I waved. "Thanks. That's all I wanted to know." I slid back in the car and whispered, "Now we can get out of here."

Jack lost no time in turning the Cadillac around and heading back to the main road. "What did all that prove?"

I leaned back. "It proved that Janelle Bourgeois was here all night, and that she couldn't have killed John Hardy."

He frowned at me.

"Look, she got back to the house there around six that afternoon. The pickup broke down. She was out here all night helping them work on it."

Jack nodded slowly. "You believe them?"

"Yeah. I believe them."

At that instant I heard the boom of a rifle and a slug smashed a hole in the windshield.

Chapter Twenty

Jack slammed on the brakes and the Cadillac slid sickeningly toward the swamp, finally grinding to a halt with its front wheels in the water up to the hubcaps.

"Look," he shouted, pointing to a shadowy figure running through the swamp, water splashing with each long stride. The water appeared to be about only ankle deep. "There he is. Loup garou! Loup garou!"

On impulse, I jumped out and dashed after him, but after the four steps off the road, I went down up to my neck. I staggered back to shore, coughing and sputtering.

By now, our shadow had vanished among the cypress and palmettoes.

Jack rushed up to me. "Did you see him? He was running on the top of the water?" Before I could reply, he blubbered. "That witch did it, the coochymar or whatever she is."

I just shook my head. "Don't be ridiculous. Maybe there's a ridge out there. Let's see." I handed him my wallet and since I was already soaked, stepped thigh deep into the dark brown water. I eased along parallel with the shore for thirty yards, and then suddenly, I found the ridge, which I followed several yards into the swamp, all the while keeping a wary eye on the dark waters around me. "See," I said, turning back to Jack. "There's no such thing as magic or voodoo. Like I said, there's a ridge out here."

Jack wasn't convinced. When I waded back to the road, he looked at me with a face whiter than my grandmere's Gold Medal flour. "You know what that was," he babbled. Before I could reply, he continued, "That was one of those loup garou things." He jabbed a finger in the direction of the Babeaux shack. "That old lady back there is a witch, a couchymar, and she put a spell on him so he could walk on water."

I snorted. "It's cauchemar, not couchymar, and I told you, there's no such thing as a cauchemar or loup garou. It's all superstition. There's a ridge out there. You saw me on it. He wasn't walking on water," I added with a sneer.

He didn't believe a word I said.

It was late when we got back to the motel. I showered and put on clean jeans and a T-shirt. My running shoes were soaked, so I donned my slippers.

"How about some local food," Jack exclaimed.

"Feeling adventurous, huh?" I grinned.

"Just hungry."

Across the street from the motel was the Crown Royale Restaurant. At 7:00 P.M., it was packed, but we found a spot and ordered platters of boiled crawfish. Crawfish was a new experience for Jack, but he quickly caught on to the proper way to eat the little crustaceans. You eat the tail, which you pop off from the head. Then you peel the scales and discard the intestine, a tiny black thread along the back, daub the succulent white meat in an exotic sauce, and pop it in your mouth. Washed down with cold beer, crawfish is a true delicacy, a miniature lobster.

Unlike many Cajuns, however, I never could suck the fat from the crawfish head.

When got back to our room around 9 or so. While Jack hit the shower, I laid my 3"×5" cards on the table and went over what I had.

Janelle Bourgeois was not involved. She had motive, but not the opportunity.

Fawn Williams was still in the mix, but I truly believed the honorable senator was lying to cover his keister. He was doing damage control, and the only time a politician does that is when he is guilty of whatever he has been accused. Otherwise, why would he even go to the time and expense to fly from Baton

Rouge to Lafayette? He could have just laughed at me over the phone.

To me, everything now pointed to Marvin Gates. He had motive in spades, a partnership and the off-shore accounts. Opportunity? That, I didn't know, but a man in his position could have created the opportunity easily enough, and just as easily, I could find out.

He could have met Hardy in Maida for some fabricated reason, struck him in the head, and tossed him in the bayou. But who would have driven the suburban to Whiskey River? One of Jimmy Blue's soldiers?

No. If Gates was siphoning off mob money into a private account, the last thing he would do was to involve Jimmy Blue in Hardy's murder. One logical explanation was that he had somehow made contact with Karen Babin's brother, Thertule Pellerin.

The idea excited me. Yeah, that first day after I talked with Laura Palmo, she told Gates I was in town. He could have contacted Pellerin and sent him to harass us, hoping to drive us away. Pellerin then enlisted the help of the two swamp rats. After all, one of them was the thug who had jumped me last night.

My eyes were burning. I leaned back and rubbed them. Not a bad little theory, but how to prove it without involving Jimmy Blue and the mob?

Closing my eyes, I let my mind drift, but it just kept drifting into the proverbial brick wall.

* * *

I rose fresh and rested the next morning. During the night, I had decided not to attempt to finesse Gates, but instead hit him head on. I hoped if I told him I planned to reveal the offshore accounts to Jimmy Blue, he would break.

If he didn't . . . well, either he was a lot tougher than he looked, or Jimmy Blue was in the scheme up to his scrawny neck.

Throughout the day I called the bank several times, each time speaking with Laura Palmo. By mid-afternoon, I was getting restless. Gates had not returned from Lafayette.

My last call was just before closing. Laura apologized. "I was getting ready to call you, Tony. Gates called a few minutes ago. He's going straight home. You can probably catch him out there."

I thanked her and in the next breath, I headed for the door. "Hey, Jack, I'm going out to Gates'. You want to go?"

Jack shook his head. "Naw. Too hot out there."

Gates looked surprised when he opened the door and saw me. He had removed his coat and tie, and rolled up the sleeves of his pale blue shirt. "Mr. Boudreaux." He glanced over my shoulder at the Cadillac. "I assumed you had left town."

I smiled amiably. "Not yet. But I probably will in the next day or so."

He lifted an eyebrow. "Oh? The DNA results come in?"

"No. Not yet. It takes some time." I nodded to the foyer. "Can I come in? I have a couple more questions."

For a brief second, he hesitated, then stepped back and opened the door wide. "Certainly. Come on in. You know where the den is."

I led the way into the roomy den. He gestured to a chair at the table in the middle of the room. I shook my head. "No, thanks. This won't take long," I said, my voice hard and cold.

He frowned at me, clearly puzzled at my chilly demeanor. "Is . . . is something wrong?"

"That remains to be seen." I nodded to a chair across the table. "But you might like to sit down first."

The portly man forced a nervous laugh. "You sound serious."

"I am, Mr. Gates. Dead serious."

He swallowed hard, and a sheen of perspiration broke out on his forehead. "Now you have me curious," he said in a weak effort to joke, but he did take a seat. "What's this all about?"

Taking a deep breath, I played what I hoped was my trump card. "No beating around the bush, Gates. I know about the offshore accounts you and Hardy are siphoning off the bank in St. Kitts and sending to Dominica. I have copies of account numbers and routing figures."

His fleshy face paled, and his lips trembled.

"You . . . you what? That's nonsense. Absolute nonsense," he added, becoming belligerent. "How dare you come into my house with such a ridiculous accusation?" He hefted his bulk to his feet, his face crimson with fury. "Why, I'll sue you for every cent you and the company you work for have. I'll—"

"Then I'll just have to tell Jimmy Blue about the accounts. Or does he know about them already? Was he in the scheme with you and Hardy?" I was certain Jimmy Blue knew nothing about the accounts. There was no way a small time casino owner like Jimmy Blue would dare cross mob boss Joe Vasco.

Gates gagged and grabbed his stomach. He rushed to the wet bar where he retched into the sink. I turned my head and grimaced. When the heaving sounds were over, I looked back around. His pale cheeks were shaded with a tinge of yellow. He leaned forward on the wet bar. "You . . . you wouldn't do that. He'd kill me."

I almost felt sorry for the man, almost, but not quite. "Someone threw Hardy to the alligators. You're the only one with enough motive, a partnership in the bank, three offshore accounts, and—"

He interrupted. "T-Three? What do you mean three?"

I held up my fingers and ticked them off. "First, yours; second, Hardy's; and third, Joan Rouly's."

A puzzled frown knit his forehead. "Joan Rouly? I don't know any Joan Rouly."

Arching a skeptical eyebrow, I replied, "You don't know her?"

He shook his head. "I never heard of her." The belligerence was gone from his voice now, replaced with a pleading whine. "That's the truth. I never heard of her."

I dropped that line of questioning for a moment. "Who wired the EFT's to the bank in St. Kitts, you or Hardy?"

Gates wiped a fat hand across his sweaty forehead.

"You might as well tell me. You're in too deep to back out now."

With a drawn-out sigh, he muttered. "John or me. We never let our secretary see what we were doing."

I considered his response skeptically. Secretaries always knew a lot more than the average boss gave them credit for. A thought popped into my head, one I didn't like. Could Laura Palmo have stumbled onto their scheme? No. I pushed the idea from my head.

He continued. "Look, I was in New Orleans when John was killed, if the body they found is John. I can prove I was in New Orleans. Three CEO's and I were in an all night party at the Chateaubriand Hotel. They'll vouch for me."

I shook my head. "They'll say anything you want them to just to cover their own tails."

"All right, so maybe they will, but it's the truth." He hesitated. "Look, you know about the accounts. I can't lie my way out of them, but I swear I had nothing to do with John's death."

"No? You know someone by the name of Thertule Pellerin?"

He frowned. "Pellerin? No."

"Karen Pellerin Babin's brother."

"Oh, you mean the crackpot that ran off into the swamp after she burned up in that car wreck? I heard about him, but I never met him."

I studied him a moment.

A sly look filled his eyes. "Come on, Boudreaux, we're both adults. Be smart. There's plenty for the two of us. I don't know who this Rouly woman is, but you're welcome to Hardy's share. You can live the rest of your life in luxury."

I stared at him in disbelief for several moments, wondering if he were truly as dumb as he sounded. "You really think you can escape Joe Vasco? He's got eyes all over the world." I shook my head. "Sorry, pal, but I'm going to turn over what I found to Sergeant Emile Primeaux of the Terrechoisie Parish Sheriff's Department. What he does with it is up to him."

I turned to leave, but he grabbed my arm, his eyes begging. "Please. I'll be ruined."

Shaking his clutching fingers loose, I shook my head. "Whatever you're going to do, you better move fast."

Chapter Twenty-One

During the drive back to the motel, I considered the unwelcome idea that had popped into my head a few minutes earlier. Ridiculous. Laura Palmo would never involve herself in such a scheme. Still, the idea nagged at me, stirring the hair on the back of my neck.

While waiting at a signal light, I spotted a red pickup with the logo *Deslatte Construction* on the door. On impulse, I called Moise Deslatte on my cell phone.

He greeted me jovially, then chuckled. "You find that Hardy yet?"

"Not yet," I lied. "But I have a question for you." Before he could object or refuse, I continued, "You've lived around here all your life. You ever know a family by the name of Rouly?"

"Rouly? Let me think. There me some up in

Lafayette. Other than that, I don't . . . hold on. Rouly. Oui, that also be Karen Babin's name."

I frowned. "Babin. I thought her maiden name was Pellerin. Wasn't Thertule her brother?"

"Mais no. Thertule, he be her half brother. Karen's mama, her, she married Carl Pellerin when Karen, she be a tiny *bebe*."

I thanked him and punched off. So Karen Babin was a Rouly. I pondered the ramifications until suddenly, a car horn behind blared.

My next step, I figured as I sped across the intersection, was a visit to Lafayette and see what I could find out about the Roulys.

Back in my motel room, an e-mail from Eddie Dyson made me second guess my assumption about Laura Palmo.

Laura Palmo was not born in Minneapolis as she said, but Maple Grove in 1961. I frowned, wondering why she had deliberately lied. His description placed her as a petite woman around five-two or -three.

I reread the first line of the e-mail again. Born in 1961. That put her at forty-five. Ten years older than I guessed. I couldn't resist grinning. She had certainly taken good care of herself, I thought as I read the remainder of Eddie's report.

The next line was like a punch in the solar plexus. She had a rap sheet a mile long, and at twenty-two, ended up in the Louisiana State Prison for Women where during a riot, she had several teeth knocked out.

According to her supervising officer, upon her parole, she had several clerical jobs, and each she fulfilled responsibly. Two months after she completed her parole in 1991, she was in a car wreck in which her former cellmate, Karen Babin, was killed.

My eyes must have grown as wide as pie pans when I read the last sentence. Karen Babin! Could it be that was the same Karen Babin who had embezzled the two million dollars? It had to be.

So, why had Laura refused to admit she knew Karen Babin when I questioned her the previous Sunday at her house? Unless . . .

I had a hollow feeling in my stomach as I stared at the e-mail, refusing to admit the next logical step in the deductive process that perhaps Laura Palmo was in reality Karen Babin.

Thinking back to my visit with Deslatte, Marcel had said that Karen Babin was a big woman, almost two hundred pounds with blond hair and shaped like a barrel keg. I cursed myself for not asking how tall Babin was.

Grabbing my cell phone, I punched in Deslatte's number, but all I got was voice mail. I left him word to call and punched off. Still, I told myself, her description in no way fit the petite Laura Palmo I knew. But then, what about the teeth?

Palmo's were broken off during a riot according to the e-mail, but when I spoke to Laura in the bank just this past Monday, she said her teeth were perfect, never even a filling.

I didn't want to believe she was involved, but evidence doesn't lie. It just waits to be discovered and interpreted, and as much as I hated to admit it, I felt I had interpreted it correctly this time.

Then I remembered the scars on her face, the ones she covered with locks of her raven black hair. Could those have come from the accident?

I couldn't help the feeling that I was somehow betraying her as I tried to figure out how to prove she had switched identities without spooking her into running.

And then I knew.

But first, I tried Deslatte once again. This time, he picked up the phone.

When I hung up, I leaned back in my chair and studied the notes on the desk before me. According to Deslatte, Karen Babin was a short woman, around five-two, which was the same height as Laura Palmo. She had been sent to the Louisiana State Prison for Women. He heard she had been released around 1990, and according to Eddie's e-mail, that was a couple years after Laura Palmo's parole.

Could it be that Babin survived the wreck, took Palmo's name, then coldly planned her revenge on John Hardy, the one she probably blamed for her husband's death and her later imprisonment?

As personal secretary to Hardy and Gates, she could have discovered the offshore accounts. Then, using her maiden name, Rouly, she could have set up her own account.

And she was a southpaw, and she smoked, and she could have been the one to tear the matches from the left side of the matchbook that I found in the Suburban.

Normally, I would be ecstatic when I came up with a sound theory like this one, but for some strange reason, I felt guilty. No, there was nothing strange about my feelings at all. I knew why I felt guilty. I liked Laura Palmo, and I didn't want her to be guilty of John Hardy's murder.

Still, I had to try to prove my theory. And I'd be lying if I said three-quarters of me hoped I was wrong.

Behind me, Jack was sprawled on the bed, snoring, a half dozen empty Big Easy beer bottles on the floor by him. I glanced at my watch. May 5. Tomorrow was the first night of the Loup Garou Festival in Maida.

Laura Palmo had promised me a dance, and during that dance, I would show her the e-mail and ask her to submit to a DNA test to confirm her identity.

At that point, she would either agree or, if my theory were correct, she would react, perhaps even bolt, but not if Emile Primeaux and a couple of his men were around.

But first, I needed to find Palmo's family for the DNA test, if there were one. I dialed information in Maple Grove, Minnesota, and asked for John Palmo, figuring there is always the given name John in every surname.

To my surprise, there were no John Palmo, but there were a couple J. initials, so I copied them down. With the second J. Palmo, I struck gold. It was Laura Palmo's sister-in-law. "Who is this?" she demanded when I asked to speak with Laura Palmo. "Where is she?"

I identified myself as an insurance investigator. "There was a car wreck thirteen or fourteen years ago in which a woman by the name of Karen Babin died. Your sister-in-law was in the same car. The Babins ran across an old insurance policy on Ms. Babin and have filed a claim. We're just trying to get to the bottom of it." I paused, then added, "I'd appreciate it if I could speak to Ms. Palmo, ma'am."

There was a long silence. Finally, she replied, "We don't know where Laura is. When she was released from prison, she vanished. We didn't even know about the car wreck. Where was it?"

"Louisiana is all I can say." And then I quickly got off the line. "If I find out anything about Ms. Palmo, I'll let you know."

"Wait, wait! Can't you tell me anything about her? My husband was frantic with worry, and now, after all these years . . ." Her voice died away.

This was the one part of the business I hated, raising hopes only to have them crash once again. "I'm sorry, Mrs. Palmo. I'm trying to find her myself, but if I do, I'll have her get in touch with you."

"Thank you," she replied in a feeble voice. "My husband, Jeremy, has been looking for his sister for years."

I never liked lying, but sometimes it was necessary.

After hanging up, I called the Terrechoisie Parish Sheriff's Department. The officer answering put me through to Emile. I told him what I had, and he agreed while it appeared solid, it was circumstantial, nothing really competent, and certainly not conclusive.

"What if I can get her to agree to a DNA test with Palmo's family?"

"She gots family?"

"Yeah. In Minnesota. I just talked to the sister-in-law."

"Oui. That sound good."

"All right. I'll meet you tomorrow night at the festival."

Chapter Twenty-two

Cajun festivals are throwbacks to the county fairs of the early 1900s: exhibits of livestock, farm goods, crafts, hobbies, and as always, displays of pictures drawn in crayon by elementary students.

The brightly lit midway usually had four or five rides, a half–dozen games of chance, and a dozen booths hawking food, everything from pork-a-bobs to roasted corn to blooming onions. Oh yes, and as always, the ubiquitous beer garden, complete with tables and a half dozen spigots filling Styrofoam cups with frosty beer.

And at the end of the midway was the dance floor, a dozen or so 4'×8' sheets of plywood thrown on the ground. Invariably, the band was made up of a couple fiddlers, an accordion player, and a guitar strummer.

Despite the heat and humidity, whole families attended, and while the kids rode the rides, Mom and Dad danced, drank beer, and visited with family and friends, reminiscent of the early days of the Cajun *fais do do's*.

Jack was instantly captivated by the gaiety and laughter. He bought a roasted ear of corn at the first booth, and headed for the beer garden.

I glanced around and spotted Emile with two deputies, all in civvies. "Get us a couple beers, Jack. I'll be right back."

He grunted. "Here, carry my corn."

So, with an ear of corn in my hand, I hurried over to Emile. He eyed the corn quizzically. "It's my friend's," I said. I offered it to him. "Want a bite?"

The three laughed. "What you gots in mind, Boudreaux?"

"I'll bring Palmo back here to the beer garden. You and your boys take up two tables at the back. When I bring her in, move away from one of the tables so we can take it. You'll be at the next table, close enough to hear us."

"Good. Me and Louis here, we sit at table. Walter there, he take other table. When he see you come, he go out."

I crossed my fingers and held them up. "Hope this works."

Moments later, Jack came up with our beer. "Now let's go see the sights," he exclaimed, excited as a ten-year old with money burning a hole in his pocket.

"This is fantastic," he babbled as we allowed ourselves to be jostled along with the slow-moving throng. "I've never been anyplace like this except the state fair up in Dallas. And it wasn't half the fun this is."

Three levels of bleachers had been erected on two sides of the dance floor. We climbed up to the third level to watch the fun. Within seconds, our toes were tapping the bleachers in time to the bouncy rhythms of Cajun music.

Cajun dancing is as different from classic ballroom dancing as a horned toad is from a prime Brahma bull. The two-step and Cajun jig are both done to the same speedy two-beat music, depending if the dancers prefer smooth, graceful movements or the discombobulated bouncing of a puppet on a string.

Invariably, after the two-step comes a waltz.

And the gay music continues until the wee hours of the morning, or until the beer runs out, or until the local sheriff decides everyone's had enough.

"That sure looks like fun," Jack exclaimed, nodding to the laughing dancers on the floor.

"Give it a shot," I said, nudging him in the side with my elbow and indicating the dozen or so ladies sitting on the first level. "Go ask one of the ladies down there. That's what they come for."

He looked up at me in surprise. "You're kidding."

I shook my head. "No, sir. This is a far cry from Sixth Street in Austin. Go ahead. Give it a try."

"No, no. You go first. I'm too shy."

The idea appealed to me. It had been months since I had danced to Cajun music. "Why not?" I drained the last of my beer, tossed the cup in the trash barrel, and promptly asked a matronly woman to dance. And she as promptly accepted.

Her name was Marie, and I figured she was in her sixties or so, but like every Cajun woman with whom I've danced, she glided across the floor like a feather as I led her through the Cajun two-step. We sashayed around the floor, and every time we passed Jack, I nodded for him to jump in.

"Why not you friend there, he dance?" Marie asked as we swept by Jack.

"He's from Austin. You know how those Texas people are. Can't get up the nerve to get out here." I grinned at her.

She smiled mischievously, dimples popping into her pudgy cheeks. "Don't worry. Me, I get him dance partner."

Next time around, she stopped us by the bleachers and whispered to a woman who could have been her twin. She pointed up to Jack, and the second woman's eyes lit with amusement. She nodded emphatically.

And as we danced away, I saw her speak to Jack, and then drag him off the bleachers. "That Jean. She be my sister. My older sister," Marie added quickly with a shy grin.

"I can see that," I replied with a heavy dose of Southern chivalry.

Marie wanted to dance a second dance, and I accommodated her, but I begged off the third dance. Sweat rolled down my back, and my shirt clung to my skin.

Jack ignored the heat and sweat. He was hooked. Between dances, he'd race up to the beer garden, chug a small beer, and find another willing partner to dance.

He was on his fifth dance when I spotted Laura. If I hadn't known she was from Minnesota, I would have pegged her as pure Creole. She wore black slacks and a white long-sleeved blouse with ruffles about her neck.

I waved. When she spotted me, she waved back and made her way through the crowd. "Still in town," she said with a warm smile.

"I told you I wouldn't leave until we had our dance."

Her smile grew wider, and she offered me her hand. "Then let's don't waste any time."

Laura Palmo glided around the floor as if she were on a cloud, responsive to my slightest lead. We two-stepped, attempted the Cajun jig, and waltzed.

I've danced since I was a youth, but never with a partner anymore graceful or responsive that Laura Palmo. But, with each step, my guilt grew heavier. I hoped, truly hoped she had logical explanations for the questions I had for her.

After several dances, she frowned up at me. "Is something wrong, Tony? You haven't said a word in the last few minutes."

Forcing a smile, I shook my head. "No, just thirsty. How about you? They've got your favorite Big Easy beer at the garden."

She laughed, a bright tinkling like a China bell. "Sounds good to me. Let's go." She slipped her arm around mine and held on tightly, as I led us through the jostling crowd.

"I'll find us a table," she said. "You get the beer."

I glanced to the rear of the beer garden in time to see Walter rise from his table and slip in the night. "There's one back there," I told her, pointing to the empty table. "Grab it before someone else gets it."

A few minutes later, I slid in at the table and set her cup in front of her. She sipped it and smacked her lips. "The first taste is always the best," she said, laughing and pulling out her cigarettes.

"Yeah," I replied, taking a long drink.

"So," she said, leaning back in her chair. "How's the case going?"

I shrugged and, trying to still the butterflies in my stomach, replied, "Could be better." I muttered, "I do have a few questions." I grimaced. "Truth is, I'd rather take a beating than ask, but I've got to."

A wariness flickered in her eyes briefly, then vanished. "If you have to ask, then ask away," she shot back with a smile.

For a moment, I hesitated, wondering if I was doing the right thing. Finally, I pulled Eddie's e-mail from my pocket and handed it to her. "Read this."

She hesitated, her eyes fixed on the folded sheet in my hand. "What is it?"

"A couple comments. You can answer them." I extended my arm, forcing her to take the e-mail.

She opened it and began reading. Her face grew hard. When she finished, she looked up at me with cold eyes. "What do you plan on doing with this? I paid my time. I've been clean for the last eighteen years since I completed my parole."

From the corner of my eye, I saw Emile leaning back slightly in his chair. "Why didn't you tell me you knew Karen Babin?"

Her eyes glittered coldly. "And admit I had been in prison. Those are things, Mr. Boudreaux, that people like me want to forget. I made mistakes, big ones, but I paid for them. I don't want to have to do it again."

I felt a sense of relief. I could understand her perspective. Mine would have probably been the same.

"As far as where I was born. Maple Groves is only a few miles north of Minneapolis, part of the suburban area. No one has heard of Maple Groves, but everyone knows Minneapolis." With a shrug, she added, "It's easier that way than having to explain where Maple Groves is." She sipped her beer and leaned back, eyeing me narrowly. "Anything else, Mr. Boudreaux?" Her tone was noticeably chilly.

"The teeth." I touched my fingers to my teeth. "You told me you have never had a filling, yet in the e-mail—"

She laughed, bitterly. "You don't know much about women, do you? Female vanity. That's all. What woman wants an attractive man to think she has a mouthful of false teeth? You might not understand the female psyche, Mr. Boudreaux, but our self-esteem is just as important to us as life itself. Anything less than perfection detracts from that self-esteem."

I nodded to her face. "The scar on your face. That's from the wreck that killed Babin?"

Instinctively, her hand went to her face. She drew a deep breath. "Yes," she whispered. "We were heading to Shreveport. There were some clerical positions open. In prison, we'd been cellmates. I liked her." She laughed softly, wryly. "Birds of a feather, I guess. Anyway, we were on the way to an interview when the wreck happened. Karen . . . well, I was lucky. Burned a little, but that was all."

Behind me, I heard Emile clear his throat, and by now, I was convinced she was who she claimed to be, and I had the feeling Emile felt the same as I. "I talked to your family in Maple Grove, your sister-in-law. You should contact your brother. They've been searching for you all these years."

She smiled sadly. "I embarrassed them when I went to prison. Jimmy wrote me that they didn't want to have anything else to do with me." She paused, took a deep drag from her cigarette, and then through the smoke drifting between her lips, said, "So, I took my brother at his word."

With a sense of relief, I leaned forward, laying my hand on hers. "Sorry for all the questions. I didn't mean to stir up the past like that."

She forced a faint smile. "Forget it. You had a job to do."

I remembered the DNA test. For a moment, I considered forgetting about it, but then, it would verify her identity. "One other thing. Would you have any objection to a DNA test? We can get a sample from your family."

Laura stared up at me a moment, her eyes cool, her lips slightly parted. Then a smile curved them. "Of course not."

I squeezed her hand and said, "Good. Now, how about another dance?"

Her large black eyes looked up at me. "I don't think so. Not right now. I just want to get some fresh air."

Quickly, I rose and helped her from her chair. "Want some company?"

She looked at me curiously. "If you're not afraid to be seen with me."

I felt like a heel. "Look, Laura. It's just part of the job. That's all. I hated questioning you, but—"

She laid her hand on my arm. "Forget it." She smiled. "I'd enjoy your company."

My heart soared.

As we departed the beer garden, Emile and I locked eyes. He shrugged. I felt the same way, and to tell the truth, just a little giddy.

Leaving the lights of the fair grounds behind, we strolled along the shadowy boardwalk skirting the swamp. As far as the eye could see back in the pitch-black swamp, tiny green fireflies lit the darkness like so many blinking lights at Christmas.

From deep in the stand of giant cypress that stood like dark phantoms in the night came the bellowing of alligators.

As we strolled into the shadows cast by the ancient cypress, Laura slipped her arm through mine and laid her head on my shoulder.

I whispered, "You've no idea how relieved I am."

She laughed softly. "I'm glad."

"And don't worry about the e-mail. No one will ever know. I promise you."

She hugged my arm. "Thank you."

"But you should call your brother. They—" A thought hit me. I glanced down at her. "You called your brother Jimmy. I thought it was Jeremy."

The next thing I knew, my head exploded, and the last thing I felt was the side of my face slamming into the wooden boardwalk at my feet.

Chapter Twenty-three

The bouncing of the flat-bottomed jon boat jostled me back to consciousness. I struggled to move, but my wrists and ankles were bound.

"Ah, mon ami. You be awake, hey?"

I groaned and kept my eyes shut, but my mind was racing. I lay on the deck between two seats with my bound legs draped over the middle seat.

From the movement of the boat, I knew we were weaving through the trees. I opened my eyes a crack and made out a dark figure sitting in front of the small motor.

He chuckled. "Mais no. Just as good you not be awake. Me, I not want to be awake when the 'gator, he take me."

My blood ran cold. In my mind, I saw the horrific

pictures of John Hardy after he had been cut from the belly of the alligator. Desperately, I flexed my wrists back and forth, trying to work some slack into the rope binding my hands behind my back.

Suddenly, a match flared, and as the flame touched the cigarette between his lips, the light revealed the thin face of Louie Thiboceaux, the hired man at Benoit's Hunting Lodge. And suddenly, all of the puzzling pieces fell together.

Louie Thiboceaux was Thertule Pellerin, Karen Rouly's half-brother.

Moments later, I felt the small boat begin to slow. My heart thudded in my chest. I wanted to scream for help, but deep down I knew that would be a waste of energy.

It's strange how in such a critical time in a person's life, he begins to see things with a clarity never before perceived. Through half-closed eyelids, I peered at the shadow hunched over the motor. And in that instant of lucidity, I understood all that had taken place.

Laura Palmo had set me up, and like a moon-eyed teenager, I fell for it. As soon as I left the bank that first day, she called the hunting lodge and told her half-brother I was coming. Thertule Pellerin, or as Benoit knew him, Louie Thiboceaux, was waiting for me.

And now, the time had come to "pay the fiddler."

Abruptly, the motor cut off, and the jon boat quickly glided to a halt. "Mon ami. You be awake?"

I didn't reply.

Pellerin grunted. "That good. The other one, he make much noise." The boat rocked as he rose to his feet and made his way forward.

My heart was pounding so hard, I knew he could hear it. I had one chance, one desperate chance. From the way he had tossed me in the boat, he had left me only one weapon, my bound feet.

Beyond the boat came the night sounds of the swamp, mixed with the faint strains of gay music from the festival floating across the still water.

My throat dry, I watched as the shadow grew closer and closer. He was going to have to bend over to grab me and roll me over the gunnel. If I could time my move just right—

He climbed over the last seat and bent down. He grunted. "Time you to go, mon a—"

I lashed out with my feet, using them as a pile driver to knock him backwards.

With a shriek, he jerked upright, windmilling his arms frantically for balance, but he was too close to the side of the small craft, and his weight tilted the small boat just enough to send him toppling into the dark waters.

"Yaaa—" The loud splash and the dark waters closing over his head cut off his scream. Moments later, he came up sputtering and crying. "*M'aider. Chere mère de Jésus, l'aide.* Help me. Dear mother of Jesus, help."

I could hear his fingers slapping against the gunnel, trying to find a grip to haul himself from the water. I kicked desperately at his fingers, sometimes hitting them, other times missing completely.

Frantically, he tried to climb over, but I kept kicking at his fingers, sending him plunging back into the black waters. Then he started sobbing, begging. "*S'il vous plaît, mépargner.* S'il vous plait. Please, save me. Please. S'il vou—"

A sudden rush of water and a loud splash cut off his last plea. The attack rocked the jon boat. I closed my eyes and pressed against the deck as hard as I could, praying the roiling water wouldn't capsize the small aluminum boat, and at the same time trying to shut out the splashing and screaming on the other side of the thin metal.

Once or twice when Pellerin surfaced he managed a shout, but it was quickly silenced when the alligators pulled him back underwater.

And just as suddenly as the attack started, it was over. The rocking boat grew still. Moments later, the night sounds of the swamp returned and the gay music from the festival drifted across the still waters.

At five ten and a hundred sixty pounds, I'm lanky, and for once it paid off. I managed to work my bound wrists down over my flat derrière and slip my legs between them. My hands were still tied, but I quickly freed my ankles and then used my teeth on the rope about my wrists.

Five minutes later, I started easing the jon boat through the swamp, bouncing off unseen cypress tnees, but always guided by the strains of one of my favorite Cajun tunes, "Jolie Blon."

Back at the festival, I searched down one side of the midway for Emile Primeaux. When I reached the dance floor, Jack had disappeared. When I asked Marie if she'd seen him, she smiled coquettishly and replied, "Don't you be worrying. That one, him and Jean, dey go for ride."

I rolled my eyes and muttered a curse. So much for shy Jack Edney. Now I had no transportation. Muttering under my breath, I headed back up the opposite side of the midway. I got lucky. Standing in front of the basketball shoot was Emile Primeaux and his deputy, Louis.

His eyes grew wide when he saw my disheveled appearance. "Hey, what happen to you?"

"She's the one," I exclaimed. "Palmo!"

He frowned at me. "What that you say?"

I tugged on his arm. "I'll explain later. Right now, we've got to go after her."

The tall sergeant pulled his arm away from me. "You don't make no sense. All that me, I hear back at the table, it all sound good to me."

"Me too," I gushed. "But as soon as we got away from the lights, someone whopped me on the head. I almost joined John Hardy."

"How you know that?"

"Her half-brother, Thertule Pellerin, told me. He

thought I was unconscious. He said the last one had made a lot of noise." I shrugged. "It had to be John Hardy."

His face grew hard, and he studied me narrowly. "Where he be now?"

"Out there." I hooked my thumb over my shoulder. "His half-sister is really Karen Rouly Babin. For the last nine or ten years, she's played the part of Laura Palmo."

Emile was still undecided.

"Look, don't believe me. At least stop her from running, though. She has offshore accounts at Nauru. Somewhere around Australia. If I know her, she's already on her way. Once she's out of the country, we'll never find her."

He pursed his lips, then spun on his heel. "Den let's go. Louis, find Walter. Den you find out what connections there be to that place, that Nauru. Call me when you find out."

Moments later, we were hurtling down a dark road with the overhead strobes flashing. "You know where she lives, Emile?"

"Oui. Now tell me what you know."

I held on for dear life as he skillfully threw the powerful cruiser around one curve after another. In between, I filled him in on what I had learned. "For the most part it was conjecture, but tonight proved I was right." I explained how she and Palmo had met, and the accident where she switched identities.

"But, how she manage that?"

I shook my head. "The car burned. One body was unrecognizable. Maybe they assumed she was Palmo." I glanced around at him. The overheads lit his dark face with flashes of blue and red. "I'm guessing everything in the car was destroyed by the fire, even their purses and identification. She has a terrible scar on her face from the fire, and probably the rest of her body. Maybe when she regained consciousness, she saw the opportunity to switch places. She's bright, real bright."

"But why she do that?"

"John Hardy. Revenge. She blamed him for her husband's suicide, and for her going to prison."

He looked around at me, a skeptical frown on his face. "You mean you telling me that she planned all this for all them years?"

I grinned crookedly. "What the old saying about a woman scorned? Hell has no fury or something like that?"

He didn't reply, so I continued. "Hardy called Palmo at three A.M. on the twenty-sixth. She met him in Fawn Williams' Jeep."

"Why Willams'?"

"Throw us off. Somehow she learned that Williams was at the convention in New Orleans, probably from Hardy who was a client of Williams. She claimed Williams had threatened Hardy, so she stole the Jeep from the parking lot at the airport, followed her half-brother in the suburban to Whiskey River, gassed up at Venable's where she demanded a handwritten receipt, then returned to the airport where she dropped off the Jeep. She changed clothes, removed her wig, the joined her half-brother for the trip back to Bagotville."

Emile didn't answer. He nodded forward. "There her place."

The house was dark, and the garage was empty. "Her Pontiac's gone. A white one."

At that moment, the radio crackled. It was Louis. "Sergeant. The next connection to Australia from the U.S. is tomorrow morning at eleven from Los Angles to Sydney." Emile looked at me. We had the same thought. He clicked on his mike. "Louis, wherever you be, head for the Atchafalaya Regional Terminal. You know what Palmo looks like." Throwing the car into reverse, he whipped around, and in a shrieking tear of rubber, headed for the airport.

I held on as we raced north. His last remark bothered me. Keeping my eyes on the road unwinding ahead of us, I said, "I don't think we'll be able to recognize her, Emile."

He glanced at me briefly. "Huh? What that you say?"

"The woman's too smart. She's going to change her looks."

He groaned. "That's all we need," he muttered, kicking the cruiser up another ten miles per hour.

Chapter Twenty-four

As we sped north to Lafayette, I filled Emile in on the money-laundering scheme and the three offshore accounts. "Gates admitted it all to me."

"Where he be now?"

I shrugged. "Probably running from Jimmy Blue."

Chewing on his bottom lip, Sergeant Emile Primeaux grunted. "Me, I always know Jimmy Blue up to something. Us, we could never find nothing, but now, we'll pick Gates up. He'll tell us what we need to know."

Just after we turned east on I-10 at Lafayette, the radio crackled to life. The dispatcher informed Emile that there were no flights from Atchafalaya Regional to Los Angles until noon the next day. "There only flights out of the airport tonight are to Baton Rouge at one A.M. and to Dallas at three A.M. From either airport, there be connecting flights to L.A.," he said. "That's it until seven."

Emile frowned at me.

"That's it. She doesn't have time to drive to another airport, not if she plans on connecting in Los Angeles by eleven tomorrow. She has to make a local connection somewhere. Either Dallas or Baton Rouge."

At midnight, there were only a dozen or so vehicles in the terminal parking lot, and one of them was a white 2005 Pontiac. Emile ran a quick license check. He grinned at me when the dispatcher informed us that the vehicle was registered to Laura Palmo, Box 78, Route Three, Bagotville, Louisiana.

With Louis right behind us, we screeched to a halt in front of the main entrance and hurried inside.

The lobby was empty. The single attendant behind the counter shook his head. "Haven't seen anyone since the last flight from Baton Rouge came in about an hour ago." He gestured to the empty terminal. "It's dead in here, but it always is this time of night." He glanced at his watch. "But in another few minutes, passengers be coming in bound for Baton Rouge."

"How many," I asked.

He hesitated, eyed the badge on Emile's chest, then checked the roster. "Twenty-three if they all show up," he replied.

Emile muttered a curse. "Louis, you and Walter

search that end of the building. Look in every room, even the woman's john. Tony, him and me will search this end. Meet back here."

We found nothing.

A few minutes later, the passengers bound for Baton Rouge began filtering in. We studied them carefully, but there were none with the petite stature of Karen Rouly Babin, a.k.a. Laura Palmo.

One by one, each passenger checked in at the ticket counter then made his way to the loading gate. I shook my head slowly. *I was overlooking something, but what?*

We stood on either side of the doors of the loading ramp, studying each passenger. Laura Palmo was not among them.

In disgust, I wandered over to the window, watching the small jet taxi down the runway and lift off into the night. Emile came to stand beside me. "Well, mon ami. Us, we don't find her."

I shook my head slowly. "I don't understand. She couldn't afford to take the time to drive to Lake Charles or Baton Rouge unless she was deliberately trying to throw us off."

He lifted an eyebrow. "Maybe that what she do. Maybe that one, she switch cars on us in the parking lot."

"Maybe." I groaned in disgust, glancing down at the private planes parked on the apron below. One, a two-seat Cessna was warming up. I watched idly, then I realized what I had overlooked.

"Emile. Down there. Look."

"What you look at? The airplane. What about it?"

"Charter," I muttered.

At that moment, the pilot gestured toward the terminal, and a short-haired blond wearing a fringed leather jacket and Western boots pushed through the door of Southern Charters and headed for the Cessna.

"That's her!" I shouted. "It has to be." I raced toward the escalator to the lower level. "Call the tower and tell it to stop that plane!" I shouted over my shoulder.

I took the escalator three steps at a time. My knees folded on me at the bottom, sending me tumbling head over heels. I scrambled to my feet and dashed down the empty hall toward the exit, the sharp click of my heels echoing off the walls.

When I burst through the doors, the blond spun. Palmo! The scar on her face stood out. Her face twisted into a grimace, and she jabbed her hand into the pocket of her fringed jacket.

I vaulted over the chain link fence and raced toward her. When she pulled out the automatic, I threw myself aside.

Two small pops sounded above the roar of the Cessna engine. I rolled over in time to see her wave the automatic at the pilot, insisting he climb inside.

He threw up his hands and backed away.

Laura Palmo gestured angrily with the small automatic. Reluctantly, the pilot climbed inside and released the brake.

While her attention was on him, I jumped to my feet. She spotted the movement and spun and, fired again. A blow like a baseball bat struck me in the shoulder, spinning me to the ground.

At the same time, the pilot threw open the passenger's door and scrambled over the seat and tumbled to the tarmac. With no one at the wheel, the Cessna began rolling forward in a large circle.

At that moment, Emile and Louis burst through the doors and slid to a halt, service revolvers drawn. "Throw down your weapon," Louis shouted.

Laura Palmo ignored the order, instead screaming curses and touching off several shots in their direction. The two officers ducked. I stayed on the ground, hoping she had forgotten about me.

Thinking back, I don't believe any of us saw the Cessna moving in a circle. Emile and Louis, like me and the hapless pilot, were concentrating on dodging the bullets Laura Palmo was throwing at us.

I looked up when her fusillade ended. "Laura! Give it up. You got nowhere to run!" I shouted.

She cursed me, slammed another clip in her automatic, and fired again in my direction. She spun and raced right into the spinning propeller of the Cessna bearing down on her.

Chapter Twenty-five

For the third time, I reiterated the events of the last several days from April 25 through Thursday, May 6, the night of the Loup Garou Festival.

Marty leaned back in his chair and shook his head slowly. He glanced at Jack, who was sitting at my side, and then eyed the sling cradling my left arm. "And you are all right?"

I shifted my arm slightly. "Yeah. Fine."

He shivered. "Lucky thing for you the pilot knocked her sports bag on the floor and jammed the foot pedal."

I grimaced, remembering the beautiful woman who had been Laura Palmo, a.k.a. Karen Rouly Babin. "Unlucky for her."

Marty grunted. "Yeah. Oh, Mrs. Hardy's on the

way over." He paused and cleared his throat. "I don't know if . . . well . . ."

"Don't worry, Marty. I'll leave out the details about Hardy's death and the money-laundering scheme. It won't make her feel any better knowing her son was a thief."

He grinned gratefully. "Have they got a positive I.D. on the woman in Babin's grave?"

"You mean the real Laura Palmo? Not yet. Her only living family was the brother. The Terrechoisie Parish Sheriff's Department is disinterring Babin's grave in Maida."

He grunted. "From what you've told me about this Babin woman, she was a pretty sly gal."

"Sly?" I arched an eyebrow. "I suppose. She could lie with the best of them, and she knew how to put just enough truth in each lie to make it seem plausible if it were pursued. But you know, lies have a way of catching up with a person."

At that moment, Mrs. Josepphine Hardy came in. Still neatly dressed, hair perfectly coiffed, she nodded briefly to us. She had aged twenty years, but she held her head high. Her bottom lip quivered, revealing the true emotions she was experiencing. "Well, Mr. Boudreaux. I'm ready to hear what happened." She glanced uncomfortably at Jack, who quickly rose and excused himself.

I didn't know just how detailed I should be about

his macabre death, but I knew I wasn't going to mention his connection with the mob.

She remained standing, her shoulders thrown back and her chin jutted out. "Mr. Blevins said he drowned."

I kept my eyes fixed on hers. "Yes, ma'am. He was in the water a few days. That's why they had to run DNA, to make sure of his identity." I decided that was enough to say.

"And those responsible?"

"Dead."

"You saw them?"

"Yes. One drowned, and the other had an accident that took her life. I can give you the name and number of the sheriff's department in charge."

Her face paled. Her voice, when she spoke, was as frail and brittle as fine crystal. "When . . . will I have my son's body returned?"

"It's on the way back as we speak, Mrs. Hardy."

She studied me a few more moments, then glanced at Marty. "The remainder of your fee will be in the mail tomorrow, Mr. Blevins." She turned and strode toward the door. When she reached it, she stumbled slightly, put her frail hand on the jamb to steady herself, then disappeared around the corner.

Marty looked around at me. "What I want to know is how this Pellerin joker knew where you were all the time."

Jack joined us. "Me too," he exclaimed. "It was really spooky. No matter where we were, there was someone dangling snakes in front us or turning them loose in the room. There was the boat and—" He shook his head slowly. "I don't care what Tony says. There was something supernatural going on."

I gave him a crooked grin.

"What?" He frowned.

"To tell the truth, I was beginning to wonder about spirits myself." I gestured for him to follow me. "I think I know what the answer is. Let's go down to the parking lot."

His frown deepened, but he followed, and Marty was right behind Jack.

In the parking lot, I dropped to my knees and peered under the front bumper of the Cadillac.

Nothing.

Under the rear bumper, I found what I had been looking for. "Here's your supernatural loup garou, Jack." I held up a bumper beeper. "Pellerin stuck it under there that first night at the lodge." I tossed it to him. "After that, it was a simple matter to track us."

As we entered the office, the phone rang. It was Sergeant Emile Primeaux. I put him on the speaker. "How you be feeling, Tony?"

"Good, Emile. As good as you could expect."

"Well, you might feel better if you know that Marvin Gates, we done fished him out of Bayou Teche. And the offshore account information you give us, we turn over to the Fraud Division at the Department of Justice. Dose boys, dey take care of Jimmy Blue."

"What about the fire at the dentist's office?"

"Gates—we caught the guy Gates paid to burn it."

"So it sounds like everything is tied up neat and proper. Thanks for letting me know, Emile."

"Thank you, Tony. Hey, there, you figure we be seeing you at next year's Loup Garou Festival?" I heard the slight taunting in his words.

With a grin on my face, I winked at Marty and Jack. "I wouldn't miss it for the world."

I hung up and nodded to Jack. "Take me home, Jack. I've got a kitten to feed."